Dedicated to JF Peto Studio Museum and Ocean County
Artists Guild.

Barbara de la Cuesta

LIFE DRAWING

Cover Art by Marie de Venezia

AUSTIN MACAULEY PUBLISHERS™

LONDON • CAMBRIDGE • NEW YORK • SHARJAH

A CIP catalogue record for this title is available from the British Library.

ISBN 9781035832170 (Paperback)
ISBN 9781035832187 (ePub e-book)

www.austinmacauley.com

First Published 2024
Austin Macauley Publishers Ltd®
1 Canada Square
Canary Wharf
London
E14 5AA

Table of Contents

Mondo

"You want me to copy some painting I did on a wall on a shit piece of plywood so you can fucking hang it back on some wall again? No, thank you, it don't belong in a shit gallery."

Rosa, in the kitchen, overhears Mondo shouting this into his phone. He's talking to some people from a Youth Art Foundation. They have called before.

She turns down the flame under the rice and goes into the dining room and blushes for his rudeness. Mondo, whose father was black, can't blush; but Rosa's people from the Sierra went about with fiery *chapas* from the altitude.

And it is that black father that she has been twenty years trying to tear out of her heart that she is forced to remember for the space of an afternoon.

Alejandro was beautiful before he turned mean. All of them were beautiful—his brothers and sisters, even his mother and father. It's what held her there in Loiza. They were so happy and so free. They carved coconut shells and they lazed about in hammocks and sang and played guitars. And there was plenty of fruit in the trees and fish in the sea. Every morning, not very early, they 'walked' the dugout boats down the beach, advancing the prow and the stern alternately, over the sand and into the softly curling waves; then stuck up

7

a little sail and lay in the bottom with a line hung over and tied about their ankles to alert them of a fish to pull in. And it was so warm, you never had to wrap yourself up in wool blankets like in Xoyatla.

Xoyatla was the chilly forest and misty mountain. The mist didn't rise off the mountain until eleven in the morning. There the tribes lived. Rosa, though she would never mention it to anyone, was a tribal person. Her people were squat and silent and hardworking. They never lay about and sang. The only place they ever sang was in church in their heavy tuneless voices.

She used to think it was the chilly mountain that made him drink and turn mean. For a time, it was ok. They planted corn and he was building their house. As she waited for Mondo's birth—he would be a beautiful, honey colored baby—she admired the way he worked, the trueness of his corners.

For Alejandro was an artist. When he was younger, he carved the long fishing canoes out of palo santo logs that his people used to walk down the sand to the beach. The hollowing out started with a fire in the center, then continued with shaping with an axe and knives. And one of these had been carried off to a museum in Tegucigalpa, where it stood up on a platform in the patio.

Mondo's words, 'some shit gallery', could have been spoken by his father. For the museum, people had followed up with offers for more carvings. Some people, like these Youth Art Foundation, who had been calling Mondo, had offered him a chance and he had insulted them.

She must speak to him, but for the time, she blushed. She blushed for his bad grammar: "It don't belong in no shit gallery." While Rosa was studying in her English classes in

8

the basement of the Waltham Public Library, to say 'doesn't' and 'any', this kid, who was brought to Lowell, Massachusetts as a five-year-old and went off to fine schools in a yellow school bus to learn perfect English while his mother picked apples in an orchard in Billerica, chose to talk like his black friends who hung themselves over overpasses to paint on them.

He hasn't seen this father since he was a baby, and is turning out just like him. This is a new sadness to Rosa. She remembers her fear that his father would harm him when he was a baby and he used to lock her out of the house at night, the fear that finally caused her to run with him to Alejandro's mother, sneaking out of the house while he lay drunk on the floor, bleeding from the molar he had knocked loose, putting the little backpack on Mondo with his Leche Klim, and finding her way in the dark with Mondo by the hand to the bus that ran just before dawn to the coast. At eleven months, he was picking up his father's insulting swear words, learning how to hammer and to measure.

Merceditas, Alejandro's mother, was kind took them in, and recognised his promise. "He was always ahead of himself too," she said of Alejandro.

She can never forgive her foolish wish that he would come to her and take her back to the farm: Which came true. He came. Complained to his mother that she had stolen from him and taken his son. Merceditas wouldn't listen to these complaints, just as she hadn't listened to Rosa's 'He hit me'. But he was sober, he courted her again, and they went back and it wasn't a month before he was again accusing her that the new baby about to be born was fathered by her uncle, locking her out of the house, bringing on the birth early with

9

his blows. She might never have seen Mondo again, as she had fainted on the road to a neighbor's farm, been taken to a clinic with a broken jaw, so she couldn't tell anyone of the danger Mondo was in from his father's drunken carelessness. Fortunately, someone intervened and Mondo had been sent off to the coast again where, two years later, her uncle picked him out from all the other infant grandchildren playing on the little beach behind Mercedita's house, and brought him up the mountain again, where she was back living with her aunt. She stifled her love for the father, took her two babies and followed her brother Tito to Lowell Massachusetts and the apple picking and the yellow bus that took Mondo off to his new school.

She doesn't speak to him yet. Just let him go back to school for now. He has just come back from jail for stealing the sky hook harness and for defacing overpasses, and was on probation. *Let him stop stealing*, Rosa thinks. To Mondo's mind he doesn't exactly steal, he borrows, he rescues things that people have abandoned and that he needs more than they do.

It was a little before this time that Mondo was home again and moved into Laureano's attic, which he started refinishing very nicely, that Rosa's little biographer came to the house with her notebooks. This was the daughter of the Mexican grocer on River Street, who needed to interview an older person about her life for a fifth-grade project. They sat in Rosa's kitchen and Rosa told her some parts of her early life. The parts about Alejandro she mostly took out except for the barest essentials, sticking to the story of how her mother had died and the three sisters and baby brother went to live with an aunt and uncle until three years later her father wanted them back and took them to the half-built house where they had to cook and clean for him.

This would be after dinner and she and little Esmeralda would drink manzanilla tea with Goya biscuits. Laureano, a man, who wouldn't marry her, but that she had lived with over ten years, would come in and want to join them. He was jealous of the attention given to Rosa, and wanted to tell about his life and all the houses he'd built.

Because of this little visitor who loved her studies, Rosa, who had only gone to third grade until her father began keeping her home to help in the house, began filling in some parts of her education that were blanks.

Recently, also, the agency has sent her to help a poor woman who had been brought from Italy by her doctor daughter and on her first day had found her alone and crying in the beautiful suburban house in Lexington. Rosa had embraced her and listened to her sobs and foreign words about a son who had died and here there were no neighbours, no stores, no church, and there was all this grass around where there should be cows and chickens at least…realising that somehow she understood. *Quieres café?* she tried out, and soon, they were bustling about the kitchen, finding chunky little expresso pot that screwed together, she'd seen before in Xoyatla, heating the milk, making coffee the proper way, strong, with hot milk. Two Mediterranean women, as Gina put it. The doctor daughter was overjoyed with this and soon Rosa was being served exquisite pastries and lunches and taught to embroider, and everyway petted by this woman she was supposed to be working for. It's because you speak Spanish and Spain is near Italy, the agency explained. But this only bewildered Rosa further, so she took it up with the little girl. "Why we speak Spanish?" was her first question.

"They were our ancestors," the little girl explained.

"I'm sure they aren't my ancestors," spoke Rosa.

"Well, they conquered us and took away our language."

Ah, Rosa feels the old defeat of Xoyatla.

She is further told of the temples, the roads, the calendars, the writing of her people, all stolen or wiped out.

She's reminded of this new knowledge when she tries to question Mondo about his art.

She doesn't see him much. He has a job he goes to three days a week. She sees him get up and shower and go off at six o'clock. Then Fridays he goes to some kind of a therapy group and to visit his probation officer. So, this much is good. But the other two days and the weekends he goes somewhere unknown, after waking up late and without showering.

"And those art people?" she asks him.

He tells her they want him to paint again something he did on a wall on a piece of plywood...

"And that's no good?"

"Graffiti art they call it."

"Art, that's what they called Alejandro's boat," she recalls.

"Art!" he shouts, "It ain't art. It's a message! And it ain't even new. I do better work now."

"What do you mean a message?"

"Oh, I can't explain it to you." He looks at her as if she isn't even a distant relative.

"I am your mother. You don't remember?"

"Oh, I remember."

"You listen to me. You father make something once they call art, and want to help him, want to give him an order for more boats just like it, and have him work for someone big and he just like you. He wants to make whatever comes in his head and not make when he feels like it, and they should leave him alone. And now you, his son, you talkin' just like him just so you can come to nothin' just like him."

"Yeah, they call it art and you gotta do it now, paint it now on a piece of plywood they can carry around and hang on walls. 'A smaller scale' they want…and they don't even know what it says…"

"What it says?"

"It has some old message. I don't even remember what alphabet I use then. I have a whole bran new one I use now that I make up in the jail. And I don't work Dorchester no more, and I don't paint on no plywood…"

She has no idea what he's talking about and is about to walk out of the room when she remembers the wonders Esmeralda told her about the old tribes.

"What alphabet? What are you talking about?"

"Messages, I can say fuck you, without no fucking eff and no fucking yoo and no fucking cee…It isn't no fucking 'art design' I'm making."

"Well, how can it be a message Without no ABC?"

"You are thinking of ABC, the only alphabet in the world?" He looks at her swamp of ignorance.

"But you make new ABC, who can read it? Only you…"

"My people read it, they read my messages all over here, all over other cities."

"But why must you hang youself over a bridge to write?"

13

"You think my people pay to go in *a museum* to read my message? The low-down messages ain't no one read. It got to be up high! It got to be dangerous!" With this he stomps out of the kitchen, goes out in the yard and fires up one of his wrecks.

"I guess you want to go live in the jail another year," she says after him, remembering how this argument about art had gone differently with Alejandro: He opposed her; he wasn't going to try to make boats for the museum people, or the business people—she forgets which—but he wasn't going to make more boats for anybody, not even for himself, or do anything dangerous. He was just going to swing in the hammock and strum his guitar. Mondo is a better man, she thinks—in spite of the fear that she can feel like a lump in her throat as she goes about making the yellow rice.

A better man, her honey colored baby, a child of the mountain as well as of the sea.

She recalls the wonders Esmeralda told her: The temples, the language…There was a language of the mountain. She didn't speak it, but her aunt and uncle did between themselves. Mondo heard it. Didn't have any ABC or maybe some different ABC.

Rosa thinks of all the times Mondo has returned from places he was sent to correct his ways; the drug program during junior high, the mental floor at the hospital when he was fifteen, then the juvenile detention the next year…Each time she was happy and hopeful. She wanted her Mondo back. Not this time. She is tired and discouraged and it has been a relief not to worry about him. His sister, a year younger, was all through high school and a year of college, in the army and studying to be an officer. He is becoming a shame to her, the stolen paint, and the defaced walls.

The school allowed him once to paint a wall beside the walkway where the old Embassy Theater used to stand. Something community minded, they wanted, but Mondo painted a picture so full of violence that had to be painted out. As soon as his latest probation is over, he told her he wants to go to New York and challenge the real graffiti artists. This town, even Boston, is not a place that he can do his best, most daring work. *Me purifica,* thinks Rosa.

He purifies me.

Then, as if these novelties weren't enough, there is the strike of health workers.

The strike could last three weeks. That's what Terry and Priscilla planned for.

She will go to Gina and her other people anyway. What can they do to her? Put her in prison? She laughs. What kind of crime is it to disobey a union? They could just as well put her in prison for walking about with a sign on a pole. The union itself is illegal to some people. These are difficult thoughts. She'll have to ask Priscilla. Where it is the law's opinion against Priscilla's, she will pick Priscilla. This thought comforts her. But if she goes to Gina that would be going against Priscilla's strike. Well, not Priscilla's strike. It's not *my* strike, Rosa, it's ours, Priscilla had said to her more than once.

An earlier strike had failed because the aides kept sneaking back to work. But this time, they said we could help Rebecca at the day center, she recalls. They were not going to make people outside the strike suffer too much this time, she does remember hearing at the meetings.

Of course, she can go to Gina without logging in. Mondo will carry her sign while she is with Gina. Mondo can break the law; that will please him. She's sure he'll do it for her.

It's nearly May already. The epic April snow cannot last. It is dripping away. Dripping from the eaves; the pines boughs release it and spring back from their heavy loads. The rich green grass of Rosa's side yard shows here and there. Only the giant dirty mounds left by the ploughs are left by Thursday, when the strike is rescheduled to happen.

She reports to Priscilla's apartment. Her daughter Solie is passing out the signs. Solie is known to run around with Puerto Rican boys who are too old for her. This is a sorrow for Priscilla.

There is a Xeroxed schedule with assigned hours. Rosa is to start at noon; until then, she and Enedina López can get consumers to the Sunshine Club and help Rebecca. No baths, no writing notes in the books; it is to seem as if they were never there.

She goes to Alcide Arsenault, and here she loses all her militancy. The dear man is holding one of Eulalie's nightgowns, and lying still in bed with tears standing in his eyes.

"You go on strike. What I do? I have no woman."

She kisses him. "You have woman, Alcide. You have Priscilla and Enedina, and you have me."

He brightens. "You come here in bed…"

"No!"

"No, no, you have to go marching, I know." He gets up and marches to a tune he hums into the bathroom to take a long pee. He is dressed, but very haphazardly. She tries to straighten him.

"You a good woman," he says.

"You got your teeth?"

This is an encouraging sign. They thought he would just give up and die after Eulalie died.

"Yeah, I got most of my teeth," she laughs. She has lost two molars, the one Alejandro knocked out, and the one she couldn't afford to fix back in Billerica, but they're at the back and don't show much.

"You still bleed, too, I bet."

Yes, Rosa bleeds lately enough for two women. Her periods saying goodbye to her.

"Yes, I bleed, Alcide."

"That's good," he says, "keeps the juices in a woman."

She laughs, and dances away from him.

"You suppose to go right to the Sunshine Club. No fooling around today."

"Ah, yes." He wags his hips and marches in place, hup two, hup two. To the Bastille, *Alons garçons.*

She sets him moving towards the door. He looks terrible, but at least he has cheered up.

It's taken more time than she's allowed and the van is impatient outside.

They all look terrible at the day center. She'd like to take every one of them and give him a bath. But Rebecca is carrying on with the breakfast and the Realty Orientation, and Rosa and Enedina clear the paper plates they're using in place of dishes to allow the kitchen people their turn with the signs.

"Good for you," Mrs. Rose says to Rosa. "I always was a little *pink*, watching all those snooty Englishmen in India and those big company types my husband worked for."

"Thank you," Rosa says, not understanding, wondering if this 'pink' is somehow connected to Mrs. Rose's unusual pinkish hair.

"If I could walk better, I'd be right out there with you. To the Bastille!" she cries, like Alcide; and now Rosa must wonder what this Bastille is. She'll have to ask Esmeralda. There's no time to ask Mrs. Rose.

Then Mrs. Hingy from the agency turns up and tries to take things in hand. But everything is in hand, and Rebecca, who is very grim and calm, takes her into the kitchen and speaks sharply to her and puts her to help Rosa and Enedina take people to the bathroom. Rosa can see this doesn't please her. Rosa tries to avoid looking at her, afraid she might start apologizing for the strike.

Wearily, she leaves to go downtown and find the strikers.

They are taking a break by an empanada vendor at the end of the Common where the railroad crossing is. The Medical Community, she thinks proudly. Frostie, Priscilla's boy, brings her an empanada. The doctors are paying, he tells her.

"How nice," she says.

"Not all of them. There's a small group supporting us. You go by our apartment tomorrow and there'll be a check from the union."

That is nice. She is feeling *consentida,* the way she feels at Gina's…tomorrow is her day at Gina's. She hasn't thought what to do about Gina yet.

A LIVING WAGE

Her sign says.

She sits on a low wall and sips the coffee. The sun has some warmth in it now.

May first, Labor Day in Moscow and other places.

The real Labor Day, Priscilla told the strikers last night when they were making final preparations. Priscilla was a socialist since she was sixteen, she told Rosa once. It wasn't planned for this day, but it was a good day. "An auspicious day," Priscilla said.

"What other places?" Rosa wanted to know.

"Well, Italy and France and Spain," she was told. Mediterranean places, she told herself, recalling the map in the little girl's geography book.

"I put lots of sugar in your coffee," Frostie says.

"You are such a nice boy."

"Some people like my mom, can't drink it with even a grain of sugar in it; but Latino people like at least two spoonful," he says.

A noticing boy, she thinks; Priscilla has told her he gets to take college courses in high school.

"You are going to be a union person like your mom?" she asks.

"In my spare time, maybe, I plan to be a scientist. Yes, I think I will be a union person. I never had much experience at it till lately." He pushes up his glasses exactly the way Priscilla does. I think everyone should be a union person.

A good boy, she thinks. How proud Priscilla must be.

She thinks of Eva in the army and studies her sign:

A LIVING WAGE

Each letter is made with just a stroke or two of the brush.

Mondo.

She has convinced Mondo to help them with the signs.

Priscilla comes and sorts them into two groups: one group to return to Irons Street in front of the Sunshine Club, the other to walk on Moody in front of the agency, starting at the Waltham Spa and turning back when they get to Myrtle Street. Rosa is in this group.

Her womb drags at her when she starts out; but by the time she has walked a block, she feels better. She's wearing a pad, just in case.

People are stopping on the opposite sidewalk. Some are clapping, others just watch. She sees The Kisser and the train girl with her flag. Rosa has to keep checking that her sign is turned the right way around. They pass the agency, which looks closed, and she thinks of Mrs. Hingy trying to pull down Winnie's panties:

I'll not have any funny business with me panties, thank you very much! And Mrs. Rose telling Rosa, about supporting them. Mrs. Rose, until she drank too much and lost her memory, had once been a famous hostess in India and Venezuela, and entertained presidents in her house. What was the thing she meant to ask Esmeralda about? She can't remember.

She sees herself march by in the windows of The Irish Travel Bureau. *Is Mrs. Rose thinking of me now*, she wonders.

Of us, of course, she corrects herself. The Medical Community, then sees herself again in windows of The Red Rooster Café.

Oh, The Bastille, it was. Something French, she suspects. She used to ask Eulalie about this sort of thing. She could ask Alcide sometime, she supposes. When there's time…when there's ever time. She thinks of Eulalie in her grave, her body ghastly, flesh being eaten away, and leaving the clean bones.

Her mother must be nothing but bones now, and no one left in Xoyatla to tend her grave. Every one of them either dead or moved here, and no school for the children, or rather no children for the school.

They turn at the top of the hill and start down the opposite sidewalk. Rosa shifts her sign around. A policeman on a horse has shooed them off the sidewalk into the gutter, and a few pedestrians are shouting at them, but most are ignoring them, hurrying with shopping bags. A few are watching them, and a group of men and women has joined their march. From the Methodist Church up the hill, someone tells her. She sees that Father Beauvais from Saint Charles is also being carried along, with a group of high school kids, it looks like. The Kisser has also joined them in his Red Sox uniform.

In front of the agency, Priscilla calls a halt. They are to shuffle around in tight circles on the curb. A small group of them is assigned to obstruct the entrance to make sure no new hires go in. It's Rosa's kind of people, illegals, they're afraid will get inside and take their jobs. A policeman on foot tries to move them along, but they hold firm. Rosa is continually stepping off from the curb and back up again. A traffic jam has formed and impatient cars are heard from.

The people obstructing the agency's doors are jostled by two policemen now, but they are firmly sticking there. Rosa and the rest of them get moved along down toward the Common, but get themselves turned around and start back up.

But I'm not illegal, she reminds herself. This lovely thought is always ready to step up to the front of her mind.

I'm not illegal. Let these policemen take me off to jail if they want.

Still, she must feel for these people she hears are eager to replace them. Their hardships tug at her. Is the union harming them? This question is too difficult to pursue while she's being shoved from behind and held back by the people in front of her.

At three o'clock, Priscilla rallies them in the Common. She assigns people to keep the watch on the agency in shifts. Rosa's shift isn't until day after tomorrow. Those strikers not parading in front of the two agencies now on strike, are to rally in the Common and to bring coffee and donuts to the people in front of the agencies, from eleven in the morning till four in the afternoon. Everyone must show up for at least the morning or the afternoon.

She hurts everywhere riding home on the bus. Lidia, Laureano's daughter who has moved in with her baby, is kind and fixes supper while she sits in Laureano's recliner with her feet up.

"Were there fights, Mondo wants to know; did anyone hit you?"

"Nobody hit me," Rosa says. "It wasn't a war. Just everybody pushes and it is hard to hold a sign up all the time. Your arms get so tired, and then it's one leg up on the curb and the other one down in the gutter and pushing, pushing."

Rosa walks by the river, after days of rain. The sedge grass, which is always late, has new green shoots. And the vines are creeping over other vines on the slope above the river. It is breezy, but the river is calmly going its two ways: The tide from the ocean coming up and the river flowing down, weaving salt and sweet, tea colored, lapping over the golden pebbles. Suddenly, at the turn just before the Mexican store in a shady spot, Rosa sees a lady slipper. They are so rare and now she knows they are threatened. She looks at it a long moment, remembering her sin of the last time she saw one and ran home for a trowel and hastened to dig up and plant among the hosta on the shady side of the house, where it died.

The second day of the strike is similar to the first. Rosa sees some of her own people sitting around, but none of them attempt to enter the agency. *They would be too afraid*, Rosa thinks.

Alcide is not in the apartment. Rosa looks everywhere. His Walk-Aid seems also to be gone. Eulalie used to hide it, but no one bothers anymore, because he hasn't escaped in months. She should have been warned yesterday when he asked if she had all her teeth.

During most of Eulalie's dying, he stayed around moping. No one thought he might go back to his old ways. What to do?

She tries to think of places they used to find him: the little park where the Embassy used to be; Mama Josie's, the used car lot on Myrtle, The Gold Star Mother's Bridge where he used to hang over and look at the pilings where the dance hall used to be. If she goes to the Common by the long way round, she can hit a couple of them as Mondo would say. No way can she call the agency, or Priscilla.

She waves the van away and starts out.

"You see Alcide?" she asks Batty at the car lot.

"Alcide? You mean Frenchy? We thought he was dead."

"No, his wife, she died."

"Not here," he says. "We'll watch for him though. What you want us to do with him, give him a job or something?"

"No, keep him here. I'll try to be back."

"Yes, Ma'am. We'll do that."

She thanks them, then turns into the cemetery at the big old beech tree with the initials carved everyplace. He showed her once his and Eulalie's carved in its trunk. They are high up now, where its boughs begin to spread. She looks up at the bank of the railroad tracks where the homeless men sit. No Alcide. Then she walks in, past the very old slate graves with the funny names and little stones for the children:

Born 1672 died 1673.

Another one lived a month: Born January 1749 died February 1749. Pity!

Then, moving on, the little granite houses with the spiked fences around, rich people. And at the very top of the hill, Italians, like Gina. Here are carved angels and virgins, like graves at home. She supposes there is a French neighborhood somewhere, none of her own kind here.

It's a pretty place. The river edges in here and there, among the reeds, which are full of birds and butterflies. *Mariposas.* They like to light on the milkweed. She forgets about Alcide for a moment, would like to sit in the grass and think about places where her own are buried: her aunt, her mother…

Of course, she can go in no further. There's no time, so she walks back out.

Then, the Gold Star Mothers' Bridge. No Alcide here either, only pigeons and an abandoned shopping cart. Mama Josie's is way the other way on Main Street. And so is O'Reilly's Daughter where he goes sometimes, too far. She must find Priscilla.

Priscilla is among the people guarding the agency today. Standing by the familiar agency, with Alcide on her mind and only ten minutes before she must take up her sign, Rosa, for a moment, feels her allegiances all mixed up. Whose responsibility is Alcide?

"The police," Priscilla tells her. One of the men down by the railroad crossing has a radio telephone. She must tell him to call the station.

"Ok, I already look three places."

She walks the rest of the way down the hill, sees it's not necessary to make any calls. Alcide has joined the strikers. He is sitting by the bus stop with a bunch of French-Canadian strikers talking French and ignoring her scolding.

They're feeding him hot dogs from one of the many carts that have taken to accompanying the strikers, so she leaves off worrying. He can take himself home, and if he does something illegal, like doing his *caca* in the streets, the police are sure to take him in. That was always Eulalie's hope—that they'd put him in the *calabozo*, instead of always bringing him home, so she could have some peace.

Ah, poor Eulalie, she has her peace now.

She thinks of Mrs. Fahey, who is breaking the strike. Suppose they send her to Alcide. They could give her Rosa's consumers plus her own. She knows some of Mrs. Fahey's baths are pretty rough and hurried up affairs so she can get back to putting her feet up and reading her magazine or listening to her police radio. If she has a double schedule, what will they be like? In, out, cold water, soap in the eyes…

She eats a hot dog and takes up her sign and patrols the Common with the others.

They're singing a song today that starts, *Go Down Moses*. Rosa sings the beginning words, but doesn't know the rest of them.

The meeting is at the Italian-American Hall, instead of Priscilla's house that week; and there are a lot of unfamiliar people there. "All the agencies are out now, and there are three people from the New York SEIU," Priscilla tells her, "an important development."

Here she's given a paper with the words to *Go Down Moses*, and another song called *Handful of Earth*.

They practice the songs. Then there's a talk about mandatory overtime, and another about street credibility. They can pick up a supplementary check after the meeting and are taken to a back room where food is being collected for a food pantry. Rosa picks up some dried pinto beans, and some rice. She knows a lot about surviving on beans and rice. At home in Xoyatla, the meat usually ran out by the middle of the week, and then it was three or four days of beans and rice. It's laughable to think about these privations in her present prosperity. Let them keep their beans. She puts them back.

Amid all this, her little biographer has been given an A plus and a word processer a gift from her teacher, who says she is to become a writer. Rosa is invited to the prize giving and sits on a little chair in a third-grade classroom next to *Doña* Lucha, the girl's mother, trying to bank down her blushes when she is pointed out as the subject of the biography to the little audience.

Priscilla invites Mondo to the house to create one gorgeous sign. "Just so you can read it," she says and offers him an extra-large piece of poster board and his choice of slogans.

WE CARE FOR YOUR…LOVED ONES

He picks, and does it in four day glow colors. It is beautiful, with colors you didn't know existed, colors that have no names Rosa knows. Like the paintings she sees in Gina's house.

"What happens if you win this strike?" He asks Rosa.

"We get more pay. Part-time get some benefits."

He is thoughtful.

"You like Priscilla, right?" Rosa asks.

"Yeah, she tries to tell me how important unions are, talkin' about Cesar Chavez."

Rosa is careful. "Can I tell you something I think of the other day?"

"Sure."

"I think you gonna be better man than you father."

"That jerk!"

"He is jerk, but he had something in a museum once too."

"Mentira."

"I told you. It's true. He carved a boat."

"Yeah."

"Then they want him to make another one like it. Do some kind of business with them. He doesn't want to do it. He thinks they are just using him."

"Probably they were."

"Priscilla, is she using you?"

"Sure."

"But you let her…"

"Well, I can dig unions maybe."

"So, you are a better man than your father. I can respect you."

"What you talkin' about? You think I should go makin' union signs the rest of my life."

"No," Rosa says, "only sometimes. Like to stay in this family…you do…something this family can understand."

"Well, maybe. But I got my own work to do."

"That's ok. Your father, when they tell them what they want, he says no. But then he never says like you, I got my own work. He lays in the hammock and swing…"

"Ok," he nods, "I read you, Mama." He gets up then and kisses her and walks out of the kitchen with his goofy walk, picking up Lilia's little Michael on the way and turning him upside down.

So, after it's all over, maybe it's understandable that Rosa feels newly important, newly sure about her place in the world. Much has been explained, except for art. Art is high up and dangerous, according to Mondo. It is a dedication, like the little girl and her writing, like Priscilla and her strike. Mondo is up above her like a kite, but she is here on the ground holding a string.

Me purifica. She has to laugh.

Life Drawing

They all have stories; Hilda thinks as she sets up her pad on an easel and sharpens her carpenter's pencil.

They're waiting in the old studio upstairs for the model to undress in the back room.

There's Debbie, who lives in her van, and believes she can make a living at this modelling business. She's vastly overweight and can't manage any of the athletic poses most of them attempt. But her bulk offers some fine volumes, and Liz, so at home in her lush body. Her breasts hang like ripe fruit. She has a shop in Belmar sells beautiful scarves. She'll bring one sometime, wrap her shoulders, and the nudist who tells them about his hikes in state parks, wearing just his boots. And the acrobatic Mare, who is an actress at the Repertory, lives alone with her cat, Purple. There's something of a cat in her.

Some Hilda can't see into.

Like the cop with his soldierly poses. She's no idea why he pursues this extra income.

Once, bored with his poses, she saucily blurted out, "Could you do a foetal position?"

"My God, woman, you realize who you're talking to here!" Lou Riccio hissed next to her. But the cop meekly complied.

A nice man.

Or that couple…

They came from Perth Amboy, an ugly older man and a tiny woman with exquisite South Asian features. She couldn't help seeing them as a pimp and his woman. They never came back and let themselves be known further.

Phyllis, who runs the group, has to go pretty far afield sometimes to find these people and some of her forays are disasters, like the sex changed people from Lakewood.

Then there is this one up here today, Skip, who sheds his robe and steps up to the platform. He's wearing the Indian underwear he promised to show them the last time he came.

Like Liz, he's at home in his flesh. Apricot skinned in summer, lying on his side, the Indian underwear a bit of a disappointment, but gracefully folded away to reveal his rosy penis cradled in its nest of curly reddish hair, calm as its master.

He has a long curly beard that only they and other intimates know about. At work and in public, he keeps it hidden in his shirt.

They know a bit about Skip because, like his beard, he reveals himself to them. The promised Indian underwear comes from a city in India where he was building a house.

The first time he was in India, it was with Mother Theresa.

He was rather scruffy looking back then. They took him for a hippy, but never speculated further.

When he went back to India to build his house, they had a farewell party for him, potluck. All the old timers present, many dead now.

Then he was away for a more than a year. They thought that was the last of him. But he was back again.

He's meditating she can see. Little smile on his face.

Hod…His mantra.

That house in India never got built. It was the drains Hod…

One of the names of G-d.

The drains had become a Byzantine problem, that drained him.

Like the problems at the Tivoli farm…That Catholic Worker agricultural folly…

Hod…

He's facing the double window. And beyond the wavery old glass the river twinkles, and a sailboat comes into view.

Hod, means splendor…

He half listens to them. Hal Stacy, the retired art teacher and that kind tall woman, Jane, murmur about their arthritis.

"This Vioxx," she says. "I read the labels always. One of the side effects is sudden death."

Hod…

They all do have shocking side effects, he knows. Introduced as Wonder Drugs…

"I've about a thousand dollars' worth of pills in my pocketbook. But I'm going to throw them out," says Jane.

"No, no, give them to me. My God…"

Hod…He brushes away his thoughts, their soft conversations.

Hal Stacy is drawing his usual competent contour of Skip's body with a Rapido graph today.

He's the best draftsman of them; and, though retired from his teaching job, still likes to instruct.

"Think of your line as an ant crawling over the contours finding where they intersect," he'll tell you if you ask.

Hilda shifts her eyes to the line from Skip's hip to his toes, imagines an ant...

Tall, kind Jane is doing him in watery water color on a piece of silk stretched on an embroidery ring.

Hilda admires her work, large limbed figures placed all together as if at a picnic, lolling about at ease, completely unaware of their nakedness, painted with an intentionally trembling hand.

Jane reaches for her pocketbook and hands over the sudden death stash hesitantly.

"I don't want to worry I caused you to die..."

Hal Stacy laughs.

Silence.

Hod...

He's told them that he has this idea of writing about them, turn the tables on them.

This intrigues them. "Have you started yet? Will you publish it?" He won't say.

Hod.

Out the window, the sail boat crosses the panes, another enters...

Hod...Splendor.

At most, Hilda knows he abandoned the plan to build the house in India. The drains, he told them.

He returned, but then he left again, to get a doctorate in nursing. A doctorate! Was there such a thing?

Another farewell party, no one begrudged him.

Now, he's back, with his degree, runs an addiction clinic. It took a while, he told them. When you go from a degree in philosophy to one in science, you basically have to start right over.

Much less scruffy looking, sleek in fact, drives a better car.

Break here.

The electric pencil sharpener grinds in the back room. There was a fight last week over the young newcomer, Tom, bringing in the electric pencil sharpener and shattering the room with its grinding.

Phyllis had to intervene. Now he keeps it in the back room.

Sometimes, Phyllis tells them she thinks she's back teaching kindergarten. She is a benign dictator, who's been doing this for twenty years. Lou Riccio has given her a pair of sergeant stripes to sew on her t-shirt.

Hilda in the kitchen, takes a knife out of the silverware drawer and sharpens the carpenter's pencil, holding it over the garbage pail.

Quieter, she thinks, and works perfectly well. Carpenter's pencils don't fit into sharpeners.

She used to be one of the young ones. Now she's one of the crotchety elders. Takes coffee, throws it out. Someone must have made it at dawn, or maybe it is yesterday's.

Tall kind Jane is urging Stacy to give back the pills. "I don't want to think I killed you," she says. She's quite upset, and he is laughing.

"Best deal I ever made," says Hal Stacy.

Skip, stretching his limbs, stands out on the porch in his bathrobe, looks at the river and sips the mate tea he's brought from home. The sun has gone under a puffy cloud and the water has lost its sparkle.

Young Matt, a teenager about to graduate the local high school whom Stacy has taken under his wing, joins him. He will either go to art school or join the army, he tells Skip.

"Go to art school," Skip tells him.

"I probably won't," Matt says. "I need some money first."

He loves these people. Their brave pursuit of this difficult skill, their frank study of his body; even if he's given a view of Skip's asshole, Hal Stacy never shifts right or left for a better view.

If he leaves again, they'll throw a party for him. Potluck, in the shabby old studio upstairs?

A new pose, The thinker, sitting on a low stool, chin on fist on knee. Hilda emulates Stacy's contour line, finding the crossing points. Like a knot, she thinks of certain poses like this. Such a pleasure! The beard and the Indian underwear entwined like a subplot.

Lou Riccio is continuing a kitchen conversation in a low voice. Some sketch book he lost, full, drawings from three years. He goes to Atlantic City to sketch the bums and drunks asleep on benches while his wife gambles.

"I can barely think about it. It's too tragic," he says. "Three years' worth of drawings…"

"She comes out and tells me she's won seventy-five dollars. Seventy-five fucking dollars, and I have to go in with her to collect. Big fuss, and I forget the sketchbook on the bench."

34

"Then I rush back and it's gone. Jesus!"

Lou Riccio used to be a sign painter. Back in the days when you actually stood on a scaffold and painted right on the board, he did a reproduction of Da Vinci's Last Supper that overlooked Bayonne for years.

Hod.

Four years reading Aristotle, Kant, Hegel. Kierkegaard freed him a bit. Then Buber, a philosophy is something you must live. Buber, he thinks, got him to India. It was where he needed to be, needed to learn to touch people. Something he needed to undergo, touching those emaciated bodies, dressing those sores. No thinking involved. Theresa wasn't a rigorous thinker. She seemed sometimes like an automaton, a mystery.

Dorothy was different. When he was at The Worker, he read her writings. She was a thinker.

Hod...

They really don't know all of this one's story, Hilda thinks.

She recalls a day she spent by herself in the old Seattle Museum, visiting her brother. An old building, in an overgrown park, given over to statues of the Buddha, once the new museum downtown was built. Her brother dropped her off, and wouldn't be coming back for three hours. Their parent was dying in a nearby hospital.

There must have been at least sixty of them, Buddhas. She had hours free, so, in spite of them being so similar, she looked carefully at each one and read the little explanatory card. Learned they were not all Buddhas, some were bodhisattvas. Reincarnations of the Buddha, a nice idea.

Hod...

Starting over in the sciences took a lot of his years. He likes to think he has another couple lives to finish up his seeking.

She remembers her pleasure at the final Buddha. Enlightenment, it was called. The knot undone, the limbs opening up, the mouth open, and thought how she had earned this pleasure by looking at all the waiting, unmoving, others.

New Pose

He unknots himself, arranges some pillows, lies on his side…Hod…Dorothy was a thinker and depressive like Theresa, but a thinker. He never met her, but arrived on the scene early enough to have talked to her daughter Tamar.

It hadn't all been a waste.

Nothing is a waste, as long as you're on a certain path.

Zaney wants a baby. Zaney is his girlfriend.

Hod, something in him resists this baby. She won't wait. She can't. He knows.

The first sailboat has disappeared from view.

Hod. He brushes away these thoughts.

They all wonder why he doesn't marry Zaney. She's so beautiful and so gentle.

Sometimes, when they are flush with money, a real treat, they have a pair of models. The cop comes with his wife. But the most thrilling is when Skip brings Zaney.

She can't wait. He knows.

Hod.

But he can't either.

A baby…

There's that old notion bred in him. That old notion, the mother thing.

The mother thing that entered Dorothy Day after the abortion, brought about Tamar, and The Church.

To menstruate, to conceive in his own body, to swell with life, to labor, and to lactate.

Not that he'd touch his male body. Encourage breasts, cut things off.

He likes to think of seahorses. With seahorses, the female delivers the egg to the male, and the male bears the offspring.

Almost feminine, his body, she thinks. Such soft contours, manly contours, but soft, padded, like those Buddhas. A soft reddish fur covers his limbs.

She couldn't see him as one of those altered people Phyllis brought from Lakewood that time she was desperate for models. Their manufactured breasts didn't hang in the right way. The carpenter's pencil didn't know what to make of them.

Last pose, upright, he wraps himself around his hiking stick. A thick maple limb found on the bike trail in Allaire. And thinks of his stocks.

Nutanex

Anaplys

Gentex

Wiping out his college loan.

Nutanex

Anaplys

They make good mantras.

Hod

Make your requests be known.

Saint Paul.

He's close lately with his parents. Helped them settle in an adult community. Close enough to finally ask his mother: Why? Why, when he was young, she hardly ever touched him.

"Oh, dear," she said, "it was a book I read. It wasn't supposed to be good for babies way back when…Boy babies. A book my mother…dated even then. I read Dr. Spock when your sister came seven years later…"

"Is that why you went to India?" she asks now, touching his cheek. "I shouldn't have believed that book."

He didn't need to explain to her his other mothers, Theresa and Dorothy, or mostly Dorothy's daughter Tamar. He learned to touch disease and death. It had been necessary.

Dorothy's daughter, Tamar, with her spinning, her weaving, her digging, her planting…Together they saw the beginning of depression, defeat. While the Real Depression his parents saw, was a time of exaltation and victory for Dorothy.

Hod

"Martyrs are the people who live with saints," Tamar said once.

The alcoholism, the drains, and the bugs. "But you can treat depression, alcoholism. Fix drains…Can't you?" He asked Tamar.

Hod

"Still those earlier days were splendid. You had to have that passion for anything to happen."

Lay your requests before God.

Saint Paul.

Now both sailboats are gone.

Nutanex is his favorite.

Go forth. Climb…Nutanex. The seed of his clinic. His clinic, his Stockbridge. But free to the poor and soiled. Messy and maternal, but with a rigor…A Benedictine rigor.

He is a seahorse, the seed and the egg in one body.

Hod.

Hilda feels compelled to raise his standing figure. Hiking stick, Indian underwear, and all, just slightly above the platform.

The Mists

The three of them, Carl Brown, Willi Ott, and Carl's girl, Blanche Aucoin, had crossed two borders on their way from Chicago to Willi's uncle's farm in El Salvador where Willi spent a summer when he was eleven.

They had met only three months ago, but such were the times. Carl, taking courses at the Art Institute, met Willi who was student instructor. They talked art in dark bars near the institute, listened to Fidel Castro on short wave and talked politics in the upstairs room full of rooting begonias in Willi's family duplex on Waltemath Street. There they planned their trip. Blanche came along later. She, it must be admitted, was simply along for the ride. Her last residence before Carl's childhood bedroom had been Boston Common.

They had crossed two borders in Willi's old Buick and had one to go to reach their destination, when the car quit on them in the outskirts of the small city of Las Tres Marias. Some street kids pushed them to a shop and they were about to leave it there and walk into town when the mechanic pointed out a fellow gringo about to drive away.

"Hi, ya." A thin-faced man in a red and black flannel leaned out the window of an old gray Renault.

"Get in." He pulled to the curb, leaned back over the seat and opened the back door with a screw driver. Willi got in front, Carl and Blanche in back.

"My name's Frank Bachelor. You folks from the school?"

"No, we just came."

"Oh, we were expecting a family, end of the month, to finish out the term."

"What term are you talking about?"

"Well, Campo Alegre, the American school. So, you're not from around here?"

"No, stuck here," Willi said. "The generator went."

"Oh, bad! Where were you going?"

"Salvador. My uncle has a farm there, raises pigs, and anthuriums, bees too. Anthuriums grow in the shade of trees. These trees have flowers on top."

"Like lawns for butterflies," adds Carl.

"The bees live up there. My uncle ferments their honey, makes a liquor from it, and gives you a buzz. You jump on a mule, ride up the mountain and look down on the…"

"Lawns for fucking butterflies," finishes Blanche.

"Wow," says Frank. "Oh hey! We spent the summer near there, in La Riña. That was a great place. I was going to teach TV repair at the trade school; but Rainey, my wife, had to be here for the baby. We have Rh factor. We thought they could take care of it here, changing the blood; but they botched it and the baby died. Most of the American wives go back to Houston, even for normal births. Rainey's upset. We're leaving end of the month."

"What American wives are you talking about?" Carl asked.

"The American companies."

41

"What American companies?" It had never occurred to him to expect other North Americans here.

"Celanese, Borden, a few at the air force base. They support the school."

"My God!" said Willi. All the things he'd been fleeing...

"Well, it's just as well. Thing is, we have three kids, and even though I'm earning dollars not pesos, my salary doesn't reach. It's only two thousand five hundred a year. That's ok for a single girl who comes here for an experience. We made out when Rainey was teaching too; but with maids walking out on us in the middle of breakfast, things like that; and another of them losing Franky, my littlest, in the market...Rainey had to quit. Then the baby. She's upset, as I said. You can't blame her. But, I don't know, I was damned happy here, especially in La Riña. I really wanted to teach at the Tech. It would have been really *doing* something. The salary was peanuts, but you live cheaper. But three kids we got," he added.

"What are you going to do?"

"We're going back. We're going to live with Rainey's parents in Radley, Missouri. I've got a job as TV repairman. In the summer, I'll start my master's at the university. We're here on a two-year contract. I hate breaking it, but we depended on us both teaching, so...When is your car ready?"

"Not for five days."

"Hey, that's too bad. You can stay with us if you want. You can even have our house permanent; we had a two-year lease, up next August, and we can't find anyone to sublet...It's ours, paid for through August. You want it?"

Willi laughed. "You got a job to go with it?"

"Well, there was a social studies teacher supposed to show up last week and no sign of her."

"We haven't got teaching certificates."

"Native English is about all you need here. When the dysentery hits, or hepatitis, they fill in with school secretaries, Spanish teachers, and housewives anyone."

"Hey, stay with us if you want. Come for lunch anyhow. I'll show you our villa, at least," said Frank.

Downtown Las Marias came to an end at a small brown river bridged by a concrete arch painted yellow and terracotta. The opposite bank was lined by large suburban houses.

"Santa Rita over there," Frank said. "Most of the North Americans live there."

On the slopes above were pitched hundreds of zinc roofed shacks. A few large tile-roofed country homes lay off to the south of them. Beyond the waterworks was a lovely green park with breadfruit trees. Frank backed up a steep unpaved road.

"Miguelito only makes it in reverse," he explained.

When he stopped under an umbrella-shaped tree in the flat clearing at the top of the hill, nearly ten clamoring kids immediately gathered around the car.

"Wash it, Mister?"

"Not today," Frank said. *Lávame* was written in the dust of both car doors.

A row of mud houses faced on the dusty courtyard formed by the widening of the road. In the center of them was a large, two-storied house, its first floor painted red, the second, yellow. Frank pointed to it. "We live there, got it cheap. It hadn't been rented in two years, too far from town. It's why we couldn't sublet. Neighborhood's bad too."

The car washing crowd moved with him across the courtyard to the door of the yellow-red house. "Your Missus not here," they told him. "She went out to the store." A large dog bounded out as soon as the door was unlocked, scattered them.

The first floor of the house, built into the hillside, included an open garage, occupied by a *pasteleria*; and a dark subterranean room, empty. Inside the door opened by Frank, a stairway led up to the living quarters above. The infants reconvened in the entryway.

"Can Francisco come out?"

The little boy was already waiting on the landing above. Frank took a basket from a row of pegs at the bottom of the stairs, gave it to him. "Bring us three *Polares* and six French rolls, and get the dog in."

"Can I stay out and play after?" Francisco asked.

"Yes. First say hello to my friends. This is my son Franky. He's Francisco to these friends who are so indispensable to him." They climbed the stairs, which spiralled rather grandly to the main floor over the garages. "Rainey doesn't like him to play with these kids. I don't see the harm. Only vice they've taught him so far is to urinate behind trees. I don't know. I think that's a healthy thing, mentally and physically, in this climate." Frank laughed. "We call those kids out there our press corps. They wait all day to get a glimpse of us going in or out. God! And if we have a visit…! I don't know what they did with themselves before we moved here."

The door banged below. "Here comes the Missus!" shouted an infant. "She bought bananas at Lino's."

"She says they are bananas, but they are *plátanos*!" shouted another.

"The Missus doesn't know what plátanos is and what are bananas! Hey, Francisco, your mama doesn't know what a banana is and what's a…Francisco, tell your mama that there are visitors. Two misters!" The shouts drowned out the dog's barking.

Frank's wife slammed the door on the uproar, came up the grand stairway. She was pretty despite her faded freckles, poor posture. Frank took the basket from her, introduced them. "They're from Chicago. How about it! Just came here. Nothing to do with the school."

Rainey, friendly, smiled calmly. "Go on out to the patio with Frank. I'll bring lunch as soon as I feed the kids."

Frank wanted to show them the house. "It's crazy. You'll see."

The stairway emerged into a courtyard, paved in terra cotta tile, whitened by rain spatters. In its center, under a patch of enamelled blue sky, was a monumental cube, faced in green and yellow tile, topped by another smaller cube, topped by still another. Built into the lower cube were two glass-fronted cabinets and a small sink. The upmost tier formed a niche with a plaster Stella Maris. "The wedding cake," said Frank. "It's a combination bar and altar. Actually, I keep my textbooks in it and Rainey washes the yucca and potatoes in the sink." Three dark bedrooms opened off the court. At the back was a smaller patio, with a poured cement table and benches, a small swimming pool, a patch of fenced-in grass, bordered by roses. It was the roses made us take the house, and the view, he told them.

The side of the house looked over Las Tres Marias. "All that down there is ours too." Frank pointed to a back lot descending in several weed-grown terraces to a wire fence

45

and a pair of out buildings. "We thought we'd do something with it, but never had time. The pool takes a lot of work. We had to caulk it and paint; and it has to be scrubbed out once a week. We all get in there in the buff and slosh the old Clorox around. It's been a great place really."

"Fantastic!" said Willi.

He could paint here, he thought.

The tile wedding cake, the enamel blue sky, the rain spattered terra cotta floors, the ragged palm leaves against the yellow walls...

Italian fellow built it, his villa, without benefit of architect, as you can see. Sometimes I think we're living in some kind of hallucination! There was another cement and tile altar in the garden, its niche enshrining a bottle of *Agua Damiana*. "He lives in a penthouse downtown now. Press corps down there drove him out, I guess. They stole his chickens, broke his fences, and painted *hideputa* on his walls. Rich bastard, owns sixteen laundries, and he won't let us break our lease. Look, here's another bedroom and another bath, and a changing room big enough for a bedroom, except no window. You're welcome to move in right back here, if you want; or you can have the whole place in a month."

Willi was looking down at the terrace of fruit trees, grinning and nodding, rubbing his palms on his thighs. He looked up at the enamel blue sky above the tile shrine ...beginning to let go of the anthuriums and the bees. He could paint here as well as anywhere.

"Francisco!" Frank called to the little boy, who had put the basket of Lux Cola on the concrete table. "Now bring us glasses and lemons and the tequila."

"Fantastic," repeated Willi. "Really fantastic!"

"Yeah, isn't it? Rainey loved the garden. We had to take it. It's all there was. We started thinning out the jungle in back, to see what we had. There's a mango tree. Five or six banana trees, pineapples, avocados, chirimoya. Press corps gets most of the fruit if you don't watch out; but Rainey keeps the dog back there now, so we did get some mangos this month."

"We're leaving the dog. You wouldn't mind taking her, I hope. Anyway, in two months, there should be guavas again. It's a fight, though, not only with the press corps, but with the *animalitos*. One suppertime, we were sitting right here, eating with the Esriols—he's a photographer with *La Republica*. Wife came to teach psychology at the university. Anyhow, a brigade of ants, a kind they call *ñocales*, marched away with a whole bush while we were eating dessert: petals, leaves, everything; left the bare stalks. Rainey sprayed everything we had in the house on them; didn't even slow them down."

Frank's two older children, a boy and a girl, came out in their bathing suits. "Hello, here comes the team. You haven't much time before lunch," Frank called. They began a game of volleyball, up to their necks in the water. The smallest boy brought out two bottles and some chunky little glasses. "*Gracias*, Francisco," said Frank. "This is Franky, I guess I told you that; girl over there—big as a horse isn't she—is Janey, and the little one is Mike, a lot of family for a schoolteacher, right Francisco? So, your Mammy bought bananas. Tell her to fry them. We like them that way, don't we?"

"Shall I get mangoes, Pappy?"

"Ah, yes. We'll have them with our Cruz Verde." Frank poured out four glasses of Cruz Verde. Carl made a face.

"Drink up, man; we've got a broken-down car and nine hundred dollars between us," said Willi, tossing off his glass.

"Give thanks for no kids," said Frank. "Listen, stay here. I mean it." Willi slapped his thigh again, looked around the garden in disbelief. Frank refilled glasses. The little boy brought him a small basket filled with mangos which his father began cutting up with a penknife, handing the first piece to Carl: "Suck on this; the Cruz Verde will go down like a dream." Rainey brought out a plate of Italian bread, a bowl of mashed eggplant seasoned with oil and garlic.

"This is terrific stuff," Willi said.

"Rainey learned to make it from my mother. Dip the bread in it, like this. My grandfather had a Greek restaurant in Somerville, Massachusetts. He was a great man. Rainey and I went to an island off Paros on our honeymoon; we ended up staying a year in a house we rented for twenty dollars a month. A great year! Only thing in the house that reminded you were in the Twentieth Century was Rainey's equipment she got from the Margaret Sanger clinic. And that failed us. Janey was born in Athens. They kept Rainey in bed for two whole weeks afterwards; it's just custom, a perfectly normal birth. When she got up, she fainted! My Rainey, what a girl! She'd never fainted in her life."

Frank laughed. "Rainey's a breeder. Schoolteachers shouldn't marry breeders. It's why I think of going somewhere else…some cheaper place to live. I think of my kids going barefoot, learning at home with Rainey. In La Riña you could do it; but, well, she's afraid. She's had too much."

Rainey put a plate of fried bananas and bits of veal on the table. They ate with their fingers, the children taking theirs to eat on the grass. A green parrot with a new, healthy plumage descended from the lemon tree beside the table and climbed to Frank's shoulder, taking the pencil from behind his ear and splitting it with his beak. Blanche noted that the bird's circular pupils flashed like semaphores.

"Roberto is a fine fellow," Frank said. "He's going back with us. Only thing we're taking. No matter how much it costs in bribes and certificates."

"He'd sooner leave me than Roberto," said Rainey.

"Listen," said Frank, "stay. How about it? A rent-free house."

"We'd pay something," said Willi.

"No, no, I don't want your money. Don't talk about that yet... You like it here, don't you?"

Willi grinned, scratching his head.

"Good," said Frank. "We won't talk any more about it just yet. I just wanted to know if you liked it. Think it over, that's all." He got up from the bench, handed Roberto back into the tree. "Hey, we take *siestas*. How about you? It's damn hot at this hour."

"I'll stretch out by the pool if it's all right," Will said.

"Sure, great. I'll give you a suit. You want a bed, choose any one you like."

Carl fell asleep on a cot in the back bedroom. There was a high window opening to the kitchen and a door opening to the patio.

His dreams came and went. Once or twice, he woke swimming in perspiration. In one dream, Blanche came in to some new strange room to talk to him the way she had in Chicago after she had quarrels with his cousin John. Though she was engaged to John, whose family lived in the other half of their duplex on Lowell Street, she lay on his bed with her

49

legs apart, telling him how she had spent a summer sleeping in Boston Common while her parents thought she was at college. Put your skirt down, he told her. He woke then and slept again and his mother was in the room. He told her his idea of going with Willi, to the place with the lawns for butterflies in the tops of the trees, and the liquor made from honey and orange peel that made your head buzz, and the mules you could capture and ride up to the top of the mountain…

He woke to wipe his head with the sheet and slept again and Blanche was there.

"Listen, Carl, I didn't know what was real and never would in that nice raised ranch in Laurel Heights," Blanche said and laughed until she cried, a kind of disintegration, her laugh.

Then the short-wave voice of Fidel Castro on Willi's Telefunken: the care of pigs, the tasselling of corn. In perfectly lucid, to him, Spanish…

Juan y Pablo Llevan un fiambre al Parque del Libertador…

The voices on the Berlitz tape.

"I'm sure that's going to be very useful," said Blanche, starting one of their old stoned conversations. It all happened very slowly. A couple sentences could fill an hour. She picked up his things, his books off the bed. "What's this?"

"Fanshen. It's Willi's. Willi's a Maoist."

"Is a Maoist the same as a Marxist?"

"No. A Maoist bases his revolution on the rural masses. Marx based his on the industrial proletariat. That's why we're going to Salvador, because of the rural masses."

"*Que dia mas encantador, dice, Clara.*" The Berlitz tape again.

"What's that mean?" Blanche asked, spreading her legs on his bed.

What an enchanting day.

"Gawd! I mean the world is crazy, Carl, and people can still say things like that?"

"I guess somewhere people still do," she said. He woke, and Blanche was actually sitting on the bed.

"Are we going to stay here?"

"Probably, if Willi can make this out as some kind of a farm…"

What?

Why did he say that? Oh, he'd been dreaming of the old shortwave broadcasts…Fidel Castro. He fell asleep again for a moment.

Blanche didn't think she'd like it here. She preferred being on the road. She'd been on the road since she was fifteen, fleeing the twin she used to worship, Jack, his frightened eyes, after he came home from the hospital, wanting her to go back with him to the baby crib they'd shared. This wasn't Jack, when was he ever frightened? She began sleeping in the neighbor's stable, with the horses, climbing into the window of her friend Sara's house when she needed a shower or a meal. Then the college in Massachusetts her stepfather fronted her the money for. She stayed a semester, climbing into the dorm late at night through a window, then, following some war protesters, down to Boston

Common where she stayed three months before following one of them to Flagstaff, Arizona where she met Carl's cousin in a diner and he took her home to his mother and left for the war, while she moved next door to Carl's bedroom and gave herself, still a virgin by some miracle, to another virgin in his childhood bed among his model ships and the Berlitz tapes.

He was shivering. A breeze was blowing in through the open door over his half naked body.

Just outside the little room, the maid, Augustina, was hanging some flapping sheets on a clothesline; and talking to the parrot. ...*como que te vas a mizuree,* Old Big Beak.

Aaark! *Mala. En mala hora.* Hallooed the bird, Roberto.

"They could take me. I work. I no sit in a tree and do nothing…"

Aaark!

"What you do in Mizuree, old Big Beak?" A sheet was snapped angrily. "They take me I make myself better. I work in a factory and rent myself a little room. I buy a fur coat to keep myself warm. I make six dollars the hour. How you think you going to keep yourself warm, eh?"

"Maldito loro. How you think you keep yourself warm in mizuree?"

They stayed a week, sleeping in the back building by the pool. "Take the house. I have to pay it off the term of the lease anyway. Four months free rent. Pay what you can if you can get work," Frank said.

The deal was sealed when Frank and Willi went to check on the Buick at the shop near the place it died. The place was crowded with cars and parts. They didn't see the Buick anywhere. A different mechanic was working, looked uncomprehending at the mention of a 1957 Buick.

"Vomit green," Willi said. "It stopped out there." He pointed down the street. "They pushed us here. Saturday." The mechanic went behind a disassembled Toyota and brought forth another mechanic.

"Ah, yes. It's outside." He led them out a back door to the muddy lot behind. There it was. "We have not done anything."

"Why not?" Willi yelled.

"You said to us, if we could get an old part. Well, there were no old parts. To order new costs five hundred pesos and takes four weeks to deliver. We could not order without speaking to you."

"It doesn't sound right," Frank said. "Ramos knows where I live. Why didn't he send a message?"

The man shrugged. "Maybe he did not think you would know…where was the other…*mister.*"

"Where is Ramos?"

"He will be in at noon."

Frank motioned Willi outside. "Listen. I trust Ramos, within reason. He's kept my Renault running, adapted VW parts for it, so it's actually a better car than it was."

"But, still, this doesn't sound right; there has to be a Buick, or at least a GM generator out there. We've got to wait till noon anyway, so we can check down the street. Most of the junkyards are in this area."

"Maybe a distributor, not a generator," said the first dealer. "And not under five thousand; it wouldn't pay me."

"I'm convinced," said Willi. "Let's have a beer and go home. I'll make Ramos a present of the car."

53

"Hey, hold it! He'll sell the parts in that car for more than you paid for it. I'd like to check the place myself. It's the only way we'll find out for sure about the part."

They checked three lots. Cars, stripped down and intact, were piled three and four high in the narrow lots. Frank, small boned and agile, crawled into every accessible Buick, Chevy, and Olds. Willi, fearing his weight on the upper levels, checked a few cars at the bottom. "Nothing, ok," said Frank after two hours of searching. "We'll have that beer now."

It was nearing noon. In front of the Lux Cola factory, they found a kiosk beginning to fill. A dusty wind blew through. "Got a refrigerator here?" Frank asked.

"Beer's cold," said the attendant, and it was. They ordered bottled lemonade for their thirst, then two Polares each.

"I'm thinking," said Frank, "you can do two things. You haven't got the thousand, right?"

"Right!"

"Well, then you can sell it yourself, for parts. Which might be difficult. You being gringos and all, ha!

"It's, it's less the language than the rosy...the rosy cheeks." Frank laughed.

"Ha, ha," said Willi. "Spare the compliments."

"Face it," said Frank. "They'd cheat you. And, well, me, they'd cheat, all of them, except maybe Ramos. So, the practical thing you could do is try to sell it to Ramos, but for a good price, or..."

"Or what?"

"Or sell it to me. That is...I can't buy it outright, but I can pay the thousand Ramos wants—actually, I think he'd take eight-fifty. Then you take the Renault, with all its. All of its beautiful VW accessories, that you have to take up the hill in

54

reverse; and in a couple years, you see, you see if you can make it to Radley, Missouri in it and we'll switch back, with maybe a few financial arrangements to suit Rainey. As for me, I'll take a clear exchange and forget who's beholden.

"Thing is, my kids don't fit in the Renault. They were smaller when we came. Actually, we came on the bus, and I just bought Miguelito to get Rainey and me to school. We squeezed in for weekend trips, but it was damned uncomfortable. Well, we could take the bus again, but Rainey's had a hard time. I'd like to take her home in comfort; and there's Roberto.

"I admit it's a damned rotten car. I don't think anyone's ever made a worse car than that Renault, and once you're across the border nobody will repair it for you. It will be pure junk you'll have to pay to haul away. But Ramos can set it up for a couple of year's dependable running, I really think."

"You got a deal," said Willi.

"Well, wait, man, you can think it over a day or two. I think we both ought to. I mean first I thought you'd be owing me money, then I got to thinking I'd be owing you. We got to figure it out calmly…take a day or two…"

"No, it's a good idea. You got the money right away?"

"Yeah, I think so."

"Good, let's go order the part."

"Hombre, you got me flustered." Frank said. "I don't like to think of you backing up that hill with all the press corps splitting their sides…"

"You talk like no-good business man."

"No, well, I never said I was a good one. It would be great for Rainey. The Buick…And for Roberto. Well, listen. I throw in the house. Ok? Till September, rent-free. That makes me feel better."

"No-good bargainer, let me get Ramos down to eight-fifty," Willi said. "I don't trust you for that. I can do it, ok. I can do it with infinitives! What do you think?"

"I think yes."

"Let's go, then. We have to pay eight-fifty. You not to cheat us, Ramos, old *hideputa!"*

"Hombre, you are a man to do business with! We do it! You take the house, you hear, and the rent thrown in until September. The mangoes will ripen again in another month and then in three months the chirimoyas. Wait till you see the harvest. And I get the Buick, and to take Rainey back in comfort. So, in a year, we'll talk and find out who's beholden, if that's possible, *hombre*, if that's possible…"

The days passed. The mangoes ripened in the tangled orchard behind the patio Blanche lay under the mosquito net smoking some stuff Willi bought from an old man at the Cafe de a Media Luna on Calle Septima.

"I'm blue. I can't get high on this stuff."

"Stop then," Carl told her.

"I'm blue and I'm hot."

"Think about something else."

"When I'm hot, I like to think about being hot."

"All right then think about it."

"Hot, hot, hot!" She flopped over on her side.

"Do you like me, Carl?"

Carl put down his *fotonovela.* "I like you."

"Better than Linda Escobar?" Frank had gotten him a little job now, tutoring Linda's little boy who went to the American

56

school. He was delicate after recovering from meningitis and studying at home for the time.

"She interests me. I don't want to sleep with her."

"What interests you?"

"She worries about such funny things, and she's unhappy in her position. I admire her for that." Linda couldn't get used to many things here, with what she considered her falsely exalted position being the wife of a factory manager, having to deal with maids etcetera.

"I'm unhappy in my position."

"I know."

"But, I'm not interesting."

"You're not like her. You're free to change."

"What do you mean?"

"You could go back."

"Do you want me to?"

"No. I love you."

He worried about her. She didn't fit any of the categories of Las Marias women. North American women had husbands and children and houses in Santa Rita; women of the lowest class worked or were mistresses and whores. She supported idleness well. At the beginning, she tried helping Augustina with the cooking, but didn't know what to do with the unfamiliar foods that the girl brought from the *galleria central*. So, Augustina continued to cook for them out of a notebook full of recipes Frank's wife Rainey had translated from *The Joy of Cooking. Pollo* a *la Tocineta*, she would inform them belligerently, plopping down the dish. It reappeared every Monday. Tuesday was *Higado en su nido de papas*, and so on. Augustina, who also washed the clothes in the stone tub at the back, and swabbed the floors, didn't need any instruction in what foreigners liked.

A few of Rainey's acquaintances had tried to be friendly to Blanche, but she didn't seem formed for intimacy with other women.

Willi, noting the fine paper and sewn pages of the paperback novels Carl was reading inquired about this in a downtown bookstore, and was told that such fine books were sent out to be leather bound by wealthy readers. This led him to little shop in an old neighborhood where an ancient Spaniard worked leather into bindings. The heavy carton board he employed on the outer pages was acid free rag that came in large sheets. Willi excitedly purchased a ream of this wonderful stuff. Next he made friends with Augustina in the kitchen and got access to the Osterizer that had pride of place on the counter in which she produced her culinary marvels. He'd brought pigments with him and his recipe for egg tempera.

"You eat this?" She cried.

"No, no, paint. I paint!"

He painted the enamel blue sky, the faded ted tile, the ragged plantain leaves. He painted the tile sink/shrine with niche holding the bottle of Agua Damiana. One day he was painting the terraces of fruit trees out back, and Blanche came out of the pool to sun herself on the back wall, and he painted the city below her upraised knee. After that, she posed for him of a tumbled cot where she afterward took her nap, or sitting at the cement table with a rum bottle in front of her, or stretched out under the plantains. He loved the plantains; he'd never painted anything as satisfying as a plantain leaf.

He drew her drowsing on pillows or sitting at the cement table eating an orange. One day, she sat on the parapet watching the urchins they called their press corps in the dusty street below. A scruffy man had come along the road from Aguascalientes and sat on a boulder to rest. The press corps pressed around this new interest which became even more interesting when the man took some coins out of his pocket and laid them on the rock.

"Ves, que tiene plata," the children shouted.

Suddenly, he threw the coins, over their heads, across the dusty courtyard. They ran, yelling, to recover them, pushing aside the smaller ones, causing them to scrape their knees. Two boys fought. She watched drowsily thinking, it's spring at home. I'm missing the spring...Her father, Harry, was locked away for chronic alcoholism. She thought she'd write Harry in his institution. Maybe he'd know where Belle was, her mother.

Willi painted using his awkward left hand. Like Picasso, overcoming facility all his life. If his left hand gained too much, he'd paint with his foot. Here Blanche shape, here leaf shape overlapping like a shadow. He loved the ragged leathery plantain leaves that moved in the breeze rubbing against each other and the creamy wall, the thrusting curved stamens like a donkey's dong. At Blanche's back, he put the spiky bird of paradise leaves and the pink crescent moons of their reverse curve blossoms, washing some of their pink over the flat white of Blanche's body. The blood beating below her papery skin.

Again, the man threw, this time behind him, down the slope. Again. They ran; again, the little ones got nothing; returned, weeping to the man's lap: *Bobos, tienen que correr,* he scolded them, pushing them off, trying to make them run. There was another fight, and the loser limped off home. She noted how the cameo blooms, which had come out just the day before, were lying now, ankle deep in the street. *Yes*, she thought, *I'll write to Harry.*

"It's springtime here too," Carl had said last night when she'd noted the fact of missing it. *Primavera,* it was called. But what was *primavera?* Just some weather the winds brought over the *cordillera.* It was wet; that was *invierno*, or it was dry, the mountains burned, the cameo bloomed; nothing to do with spring, with seedlings in the window, with that tremendous cranking over the whole tremendous machinery that made the sun go down hours later or earlier. Here the sun set every day at six.

She would write to Harry.

Again, the man threw. Half of the children were in tears, the other half crowing over their mounting stores of *centavos.* Why does he do it? She felt depressed. The man was evil. His money was evil. Where there was hardship he was spreading misery. She scratched a mosquito bite thinking, yes she would write. At least, you always knew where Harry was. Last she'd known of Belle she was in St. Louis married to a man who owned a salon for treating baldness; but that marriage, she knew from Harry, was over in 1962. Belle had moved alone to somewhere in the East.

And Jack, no, she can't think of Jack yet. Jack diving backward into the pool, Jack skiing on the hardest trails and teaching himself. He never needed instructors. Until…No, don't think.

Again, the man threw. *"Corran babosos,"* he called turning his pockets out. *He would have done better buying himself a pair of shoes*, she thought noting his flapping soles.

The hair salon husband, unlike poor Harry, had been rich. Maybe Belle had something from him, could spare her something. She'd feel better if she had a bit of money her own.

"Los grandes quedan con todo!" wailed a child, throwing herself on the grass under where Blanche sat. *Poor child*, she thought. What if she were to drop her a coin? But no! It would only make things worse. Such a pretty little girl, with fine features, a fat little belly glimpsed through her torn dress, nice sturdy little legs though covered with dust. *I would love a child,* she thought. *I would adopt one of these if Carl won't let me have one. Then I would be happy. It's what I need to make me happy.*

After Willi was finished, she fell asleep in the chaise. Willi, pleased with his morning's work, sweated over his lunch, sharing Augustina's mess of rice and beans, then had a cigar and a short nap before going to the print shop. He got the job there after weeks of pestering them: His father had an old Chandler Price press in the basement, taught him how to run it. At the shop, they still used that same old model. Their belt needed cleaning, he told them, he could fashion a pin for one that was missing…All in his laughable Spanish. Finally, they agreed to a miserable salary.

"No sirve!" said Zamora. The ink was wrong for the coated paper they were using. Cutting it with linseed oil blurred the photo engraving. *No importa*, no *importa*. It was only a political poster; but Willi wasn't happy, found some dusty cans of ink in the store room. They wasted an hour; the cans had no labels. Willi sorted them after a fashion. Don't

matter, Zamora reiterated. He found one that served, but it was green. They ran it; Hugo, still faster than Willi, put through three hundred in two hours. Willi took over, ran two hundred. They'd get it done by next afternoon: *Bueno, bueno.* They cleaned off plate and rollers, covered the wells with a sheet of plastic. He hated clean-up, a job his father used to leave to him. It would be more efficient to run shifts till they were finished, but Zamora liked to close up, roll down the iron grille.

"Pretty, the green," said Zamora, hanging one up: PROGRESO & EMPLEO, Ruiz Nogales. Shifty green face. The floor was spread with them. They left and stopped for a Cruz Verde in the cantina at the corner. Zamora talked about the new offset presses. Trouble was the Chandler Price still paid.

"You ever want to sell it, I'll buy it," Willi said.

"What would you do with it?"

"Wood engravings, like the old days."

"No call for it," Zamora said.

At Frank and Rainey's farewell party, Frank led someone up to him, and Carl stood to shake hands with an older gentleman wearing a suit and tie.

"Rafael Villegas," Frank said. "His nephew is in my history class."

"Encantado, yes," said Sr. Villegas. "It is a shame, I admit, that I send my sister's child to your school. He will go to MIT, I hope, and study mining, as I did, and spend his life most likely in a place like Colorado, thus depriving this benighted country further of its professional class; but one must think of the child, yes."

Carl moved with Sr. Villegas over to the back wall of the patio. "MIT is a very good school," Carl said.

"Yes," said Sr. Villegas. "And there is the Colorado School of Mines. That is my Alma Mater. The mother of my soul, ha, ha! I was unfortunately brought up to believe these mountains were the mothers of my soul..." He waved his hands off to the north where the *cordillera* glowed lavender in the sunset. "Are you familiar with the Colorado School of Mines?"

"Well, no. I went to a very small church college. It was founded by my ancestors, so I was given a scholarship. I studied literature, things like that."

"Ah, literature." Sr. Villegas put his punch glass down on the parapet with an elegant gesture and accepted a crust spread with *baba ganoush* from Rainey. "My wife is a lover of literature. She reads English. She longs to speak English well. You must meet her."

He gave Carl his card. He was president of Cementos Valle. *Perhaps it could be parlayed into a job*, he thought, *putting it carefully into his shirt pocket*.

The mountains burned, the soot settling on the white tablecloth of the patio table. The chirimoyas ripened. Augustina taught Blanche to cook rice and to soap their clothes in the cement tub and lay them on the grass in the noonday sun to bleach. When Willi got a little raise, they decided they could keep her on for two days a week, after Frank left. She could keep her room and work for the neighborhood the other five days.

Don Rafa was pleased to get a note in the mail from Carl. His offices were not in the plant but downtown on the Avenida Lugo. Carl must pay him a call.

He went on foot on Monday morning and found the office on the third floor of the Edificio Zacour, which stood up painfully between two bulldozed remains of neighboring buildings that had never been rebuilt following an earthquake in '61. There was a tank at the corner, and a soldier posted in the doorway. The presidential votes were still being counted.

"So, you are a young man who loves literature?" *Don* Rafa got up from behind his desk and came around to shake Carl's hand. "I always go at this hour to the café downstairs. You will come?"

Café Candelaria roared like the surf. The doors to the street were all open, and from a helicopter overhead a voice was broadcast counselling calm: calm! Cried Don Rafa raising a fist.

"A cretin calm, the people are in love with calm, even the young men. When I think of myself at twenty, at twenty-four, sitting up all night among journalists and desperate men plotting assassinations…You, what do you think of such calm?"

"Well, I'm not too interested in politics," Carl said. "Are things really very dangerous?"

"No, it is merely, if there is a change of government, some workers for the state electric, and so forth, lose their jobs to people of the opposing party. It is simple self-interest. And of course, the count takes nearly a month, so during that time everyone sits up all night to worry and dispute. So, you are not interested in politics. What is your interest then? What did you expect to find in this cursed place?"

"I don't know…some space, some…" He thought of the afternoons he spent with Willi in the dark bar on Canning Street, Willi nursing bottles of dark ale and a growing grudge against the country his German Socialist father had chosen to emigrate to in the Forties. Like this café, there were newspapers spread across the tables, and loud talk at the bar. Here it was louder, like the surf.

"Explain it to me. I don't understand." Don Rafa made a gesture towards a waiter, who came and took an order for *café tinto* and *aguardiente* with a dish of limes.

"Well, my friend Willi is looking for what he might call 'real'...real work...Farming, raising pigs, planting...I can't explain it very well. And of course, he wants to paint."

"And you?"

He wanted to say that perhaps he was looking for beauty, for goodness...but it was a much too embarrassing thing to say. He had read a good bit of Tolstoy in the past year, and thought of himself as a type of Levin.

THE PEOPLE MUST AWAIT IN CALM...

The voice from the sky caused the roar to cease.

"Ah, yes! We are to wait calmly with tanks in the streets," jeered Don Rafa. "Yes, you were saying..."

Just some space...Carl struggled with his thought. "Some clarity...to begin my life."

"Some clarity! Ah, dark, dark it would have to be for someone to come here looking for light," cried Don Rafa. "Aye, I'm an old man..."

THE RESULTS OF TODAY'S ELECTION, WHICH WILL BE...

"Not so old I don't remember, no. Once I read poetry. When we were not plotting assassinations, we read poets and walked into the streets at dawn, haggard and ecstatic, yes! But then he died in his bed…"

"Who was that?" Carl asked.

"The villain we planned to assassinate…!"

THERE WILL BE NO MILITARY COUP…

"Twelve years we talked…Aye, perhaps you are right in not caring for politics. I had a cousin once, became very rich. He used to say to me, 'What is this running with journalists and going to jail?'"

"I love this accursed country," I said. "I want to save it."

"To save it, oh God! I was twenty-three."

"It doesn't do, perhaps," he went on, waving again for the waiter. "It doesn't do to love an entire people…"

WE REPEAT, NO MILITARY COUP…

"Aye, caray, these elections, six weeks to count the ballots. What kind of a country is this? The devil's own, but what was I saying? Ah yes, one must learn to love what one possesses, my cousin told me, 'A wife, a son…He has five sons. I have none. But his meaning is the same: To love one's own life and want to begin it, as you do.'"

The waiter came with the order. The volume of talk surged to overcome the drone of the helicopter each time it passed overhead.

"He became very rich, this cousin of mine. He put all his sons through university abroad. The last son, I remember, told his father he wished to study law at the Universidad Nacional, that this was a good starting-out point for any career. Well, to this my cousin replied, 'The best starting out point, *mihijo*, the best starting out point is aboard an international flight at Chiapitas International Airport!' How about that, eh?" *Don* Rafa clapped Carl on the shoulder and downed his *café tinto* in one gulp.

THE GOVERNMENT COUNSELS CALM AND PATIENCE.

The helicopter was moving off to another part of the city.

"Ah yes, calm, calm and patience when it takes a month and a half, the counting! In your country they have the voting machine even in the smallest village. No need to wait with tanks in the streets. No wonder there are plots. So, you are a teacher of English."

"No, no. I just thought your wife would desire some conversation…we might read things and talk about them after."

"Mrs. MacWhirter tells me you are a fine teacher." The fact that Don Rafa knew Linda MacWhirter was Carl's first indication of how interwoven was the life of the city.

"She is too kind, but I might help someone, I suppose, to learn English."

"My wife has all her afternoons free. You will come on Friday to make arrangements, yes."

"Yes, yes, I'll be happy to."

"She is an idle woman like them all, but intelligent. She amuses herself with languages. We shall see. I'm quite sure you will serve."

Don Rafa lived in Barrio Santa Rita and always walked home at nightfall. Carl walked with him up the Calle Quinta, as it was his way home too, and they cut through the water works, climbing the path that circled the treatment plant, and pausing at the top of the hill to look down on Las Marias.

"Used to come up here and fly huge muslin kites shaped like buzzards when I was a boy. When they'd break loose, they'd fall into the palms of the Plaza Central...Ah, yes. Just look at all those lights, not a flicker." The sun had just sunk behind the Cordillera Oriental and the lights of San Fernando were winking on. "'If you didn't know it was Las Marias, you might think it was Paris,' as my old friend Feliciano Bustamante used to say, and we'd remember how twenty years ago they hadn't the hydroelectric and all that side was dark."

"Ah, yes. It was Feliciano and I put the power plant in, in 1942, it was. 'Is that San Roque over there?' he'd say. 'That it is,' I'd say. Used to be the Jesuit seminary was as far as San Roque went."

"My wife, Lucita wanted to buy a lot out there in 1950. If I'd bought two or three...be a millionaire today...She has a good head for a woman, I have to admit. But then, it could have happened the city spread to the east...God, to think that thirty years ago they had no electric power there's that fellow in Chocó sending up a satellite. True, it was in the newspaper. He's made a launching pad of bamboo. Lucita read it. Not going to be able to send it up, though. There's a bunch of women's organizations objecting to the monkey..."

"Monkey...?"

"They wanted to send up a monkey, the poor wretch, but the women's organizations have the monkey *incommunicado* in Los Olmos, and a court order to have the poor fellow undergo a psychiatric examination, hah! hah! It's what happens to the scientific impulse here. Well, you go that way, I go this, until Friday then."

The following Friday, Carl followed Don Rafa's directions to the opposite side of the city. Some large new buildings set well back from the street behind gates housed the Canadian and the Spanish consulates. The Villegas house and some other older houses were halfway up the hill and flush with the street. Backing Miguelito up this hill was a bit more embarrassing than negotiating the hill at home.

An elderly woman opened the door for him. *She was not*, as Carl thought, *a maid, but Don Rafa's sister*. He was led back through a series of rooms to a dark study where Doña Luz sat behind a large table. She stood and stretched out both arms to approach him, laying them on his arms to show a certain warmth, but also, he thought, to fend off the habitual double kiss of greeting.

She was a tall fragile woman but for a certain haggardness around her eyes, looked to be much younger than her husband.

"I must show you around, the garden…" She spoke and moved a little awkwardly, probably being unused to using English; but opening the doors to the deep garden behind the study and walking onto its paths seemed to restore her to naturalness. They were two people who would not normally meet, he thought, and she was seeking to smooth the way by showing him something she obviously loved.

"My camellias," she said, plucking off dead blossoms here and there from the rectangular beds and cupping them in her large bony hand. They were an extraordinarily deep coral and at the height of their blooming.

"Lovely," Carl said.

"Are they not? It is fine summer for them."

"Summer…?"

"Well, we call the dry season the summer. Winter is when it rains in February and again in October."

"Ah."

Her hand was full of the crumpled blossoms and she laid them on a cement bench. "*Flores marchitas*," she said. "How is it said in English?"

"Withered flowers, it's nicer in Spanish."

She became uneasy under his gaze. "But let us go back. You must see also the library."

They returned to the dark study and when his vision recovered from the intense light of the garden he saw that three walls were lined floor to ceiling with books. They seemed to be in several languages, mostly French. "You must take any book you wish," she said.

"You are very kind."

"Look them over, perhaps you will see something."

There were translations of English authors: Dickens, Thackeray, Fielding, bound in red leather; unbound French classics printed on creamy paper. He noticed Henry Adams' *Mont Saint-Michel and Chartres,* and took this out.

"You must borrow it," she said.

"I've read it."

"Oh, then perhaps something else."

"No, no, I meant it's one of my favorite books…"

"Ah, so. A friend gave it to me. We saw the cathedrals together. I read some of it. It is difficult."

"We might read it together."

"Yes, yes, I should like it. We can study right here in this room." She drew shut another blind that was allowing a tiny patch of sun on the rug, and turned on a floor lamp.

"You speak English very well," he said.

"Ah, no. I learn only a little with Mrs. Galloway the doctor's wife. She has gone back to Tennessee with her family; so I look for you…"

"Next week, this same day at three thirty I am free," he said.

"That is good."

"I've never taught before."

"But Mrs. McWhirter speaks very well of you."

"She is too kind. You are too kind."

"You will come next week then." She walked him to through an airy dining room to the door. And you must take the book. He still had the Henry Adams in his hand.

"Tell me," he said, "Have you seen Chartres?"

"Oh, yes, and you?"

"Never."

"You must, some day."

He thought of his new relationship to his country and the improbability of ever travelling anywhere.

"Yes, yes, but tell me," he said, "did you see it first or read the book first?"

"I saw the cathedrals first. She picked some blown peonies out of a bunch on a table beside the door, held them in her hands as she had held the camellias."

"Then you must go back," he said.

"Ah, no…"

Couldn't you? He thought of her as rich, free to do as she wished.

71

"No," she said quite finally. "I marry; I come here. This is my life."

"But you have never wished to go again?"

"No," she said, "I have never wished to change what has been." She smiled and gave him her hand, until next week, then.

Yes, yes, he carried off the book.

Rereading the Henry Adams mornings on the patio was a new pleasure. The book was bound in leather and had thick creamy pages that, after page 60, had to be opened with his penknife. And no one was going to ask him to write a sophomoric paper on it or ask his callow opinion. He would reread all his college books, he resolved. Here under a wood rose vine. And discuss them in a leisurely, adult way with this woman who had left him with an initial impression of her long, stooped body, her intelligent eyes, and her bony cupped hands holding the fading blossoms, *Flores marchitas*.

At the end of June the family left in the Buick, the roof piled high with luggage, and with Roberto in his cage. As the car bumped down the hill, the three of them and Augustina leaned over the parapet to wave goodbye.

"They might have taken me," she wailed.

Every day was the same as the one before. That was what Willi liked. Every day the same plunge into work. Only Blanche's poses changed, and his thinking about his line.

A slow line, Willi thought. Thoughtful, hesitant line, dividing Blanche substance from concrete substance, and leaf substance. Slow, see what slow can do. Overcome facility, Picasso, overcoming facility all his life. Slow, slow; this side, leaf and flower, this side, girl.

"Why do you look at me like that?" Blanche asked.

His uninstructed left hand, when it gains too much art, he'll hold it in his toes. No shadow, no mass, just this line… Can you hold it just another minute. She had a wonderful shape, long necked, long waisted. The shredded banana leaves lifted in the breeze with a leathery sound. The press corps were in the subterranean garage again, shrieking with laughter.

"You like me," Willi?

"Sure."

"I mean in a certain way."

"I don't like complications."

"There wouldn't have to be."

She hadn't had a period for two months. *But that was because of the change of water*, she thought.

Between the two of us we can't make her happy, Willi was thinking.

"Carl never gets back till three."

"I'll take you to the Tertulia for a Cruz Verde."

"All right." She jumped up and put on her skirt.

The Tertulia roared with talk. They took an inside table as the sidewalk tables were filled. Willi was happy. His work that morning felt like victory. Blanche caused stares when she walked in; women didn't come here. Clodo Gomez, whom Willi knew from the neighborhood, came and sat with them, bringing his racing paper and spreading it on the table.

"Let me initiate the little Miss. You will see; betting is divine when you put your mind to it, but only the favorites at the start. Start out with the favorites. One must have a system."

"A system?"

"Yes," said a man reading at the next table. The Tertulia lent out cheap paperback books: collections of poetry, manuals on hypnotism and sexual techniques, *fotonovelas*.

Pepe Joroba came in. Pepe Joroba was forty-two years old and had written twenty-three plays. Willi had met him at a party at the print shop, when one of his plays, which they printed for him, came out. Clodo ordered another round of Polares. "Sit down, sit down."

The helicopters were still overhead, but people hardly noticed in this the third week of the counting of election results.

WE REPEAT, WE REPEAT, CITIZENS HAVE NOTHING TO FEAR FROM THE PROTECTORS OF THE FATHERLAND…

"Someone should write a play about this election," Willi said.

"I think I have," said Pepe Joroba. I wrote a play set in the courtyard of this family works for the electric company. They're all gathered around drinking, listening to the radio night after night, waiting for the election results; because, you see, if the other party gets in the father will lose his job… not set here, of course; here we have the glorious Civil Service.

"Byzantium itself," said Clodo.

"You're right. But back in '53, everyone was a political appointee. It was worse."

"Shall I put Senador or Miel de Abeja for the second choice?" asked Blanche.

"One's as bad as the other. Put Mi Colonel."

"Teachers were the ones made all the trouble. The intellectual proletariat," said Pepe.

"There's nothing for it but to put the top favorite in the third. The fourth you can play around a little. There's Bizcocho and Cruz Verde."

"The intellectual proletariat," went on Pepe. "Thin soup that lot nothing, but chalk dust in their pockets, even today." He ordered another round of Polar Beer.

"What do you say? Gemelo or Papel Sellado in the fifth?" asked Clodo.

"Gemelo," Willi said. He didn't know anything about horse racing, but he liked the name.

"That's the favorite," said Clodo. "Gives you four favorites, that's too many. I never put more than three. You put more you divide the pot with fifty thousand other *miserables*."

"Let me choose," Blanche said. He passed her the form. "Bicho looks good."

"Bicho it is. The ladies have a gift. I ever tell you I win the *Cinco y Seis* twice? The first time I got so excited I got married and made five children before I came to my senses. Second, I would have won, I should say, but I forgot to file the form, and with only three favorites. I considered shooting myself. Nothing is worse than regret. Don't let anyone tell you otherwise."

"Ah, well, one lives in hope," said Clodo.

A cavalcade of army trucks passed, their tarps flapping.

Yes, one lives in hope. With the lottery, I have a method. I play the end numbers, regular, each week. That way you are bound to win, one or two hundred pesos a month. The money

I win I play on the whole number. One lives in hope, yes! *jugar es divino!*

CITIZENS SHOULD MAINTAIN CALM...

"The voice was overhead again. Good Lord," Willi said. "I thought it was over."

"It takes at least another week," said Clodo.

THE AIR FORCES WISH TO ASSURE CITIZENS OF THEIR NEUTRALITY.

"I want another, *Cinco y Seis,*" Blanche said.

"Allow me," said Clodo Gomez, and, taking a ten peso bill from his wallet, he sent the shoeshine boy to the corner tobacco store. Blanche tried to pay him but he waved her off.

PEOPLE SHOULD REMAIN IN THEIR HOUSES AWAITING THE RESULTS...

Remain in our houses indeed!

"Yes, this play. I had two endings," said Pepe. "I could never decide if I wanted it to end well or bad. One of them was they win...their party wins. The hero will keep his job, so they have this wild final party with fireworks and radios blaring, all on stage. I remember something like it really happened in my neighborhood. Only it was a water commissioner's assistant...lived back of me, kept me awake night after night, e*n visperas.*"

"The other ending was tragic, twelve kids and no job. I don't remember which I decided on. I have a difficult time knowing if my muse is tragic or comic."

Willi bought a round, and Blanche filled out another card with no favorites, and they walked back, past the *por puesto* drivers, waiting on the Avenida Sexta for four fares so they could head out full for Rionegro, through the waterworks, and up the long hill home. I'm going to play the horses every week, Blanche said. Belle would like the idea. She tapped the acacia leaves overhead into tiny fists. The city smelled of black beans, a thousand evening meals cooking.

She hadn't had a period for six weeks now. But that had happened to her before, on the road, not eating well, only this funny brown spotting. There was something wrong with her. Maybe it was cancer.

Blanche, Carl thought, *desirable Blanche, who'd come to his childhood bed and given herself to him on this same bed, among his books and model ships*. He felt her unhappiness.

If they'd been at home, would she have long since moved on, hitchhiked on across the country? Here, to behave in her old free and easy way, was unthinkable. Here, they lived in the house of a laundry tycoon. He read Luz Villegas' handsome editions from Spain and Argentina. They were vaguely upper class, if they could be classified at all. The upper classes, here, didn't drop out and employ themselves as gardeners and bricklayers.

"Maybe she should have a child," Willi said. "A child would amuse her."

"What do you think?" Carl asked him.

"I don't think much of the idea, frankly. A child isn't a pet."

77

"True."

"Do you mean personally…a child of mine, or any, any child?" Willi asked.

"Both."

"Well, personally, I consider I'm the end of my family. I've always felt that. I. was the only one. No sisters and brothers, no first cousins either side, my mother over forty when I was born. An exhausted line, families die. I've always looked on myself that way, an end…the one to express it all maybe, all the armchairs and China cupboards and pot roasts and cabbage soups…press it all into some kind of shape and make an end…

"And as to *any* child; well, we're an exhausted empire is my opinion, the end of a line. One or two more generations, what do they mean? Better to use the opportunity to protest, make a statement, make art, I say."

Willi had talked Zamora into letting him come in an extra afternoon and print his woodcuts of Blanche posing on the patio wall. Using the tail ends of ink cans that Zamora threw out because they weren't enough for a run, he ran the lighter colors first, Blanche's lounging body; then cutting away so the figure stayed light as he ran the darker enamel blue of the sky, pink of the reverse curve of the bird of paradise blooms, terra cotta of the wall, green of the spiky leaves, and then burnt sienna for the outlines that were all that were left behind on the board. He could have done it all by hand but with the Chandler Price he ended up with twenty prints, which he signed and numbered.

Making do with Zamora's neglected equipment, he thought of his father, the Bavarian socialist, who used to go through the neighbors' trash to find things he could make useful again.

Carl always asked Blanche, if she had her diaphragm in, and usually she did, only now and then, about one night in ten, say, she left it out and lied to him. It was like a recurring need with her, deceiving people. It made life flavorful; taking a chance like this was like playing the lottery. Besides it wasn't much of a risk, she'd thought; "she was probably sterile, her mother had a friend who was sterile because of her periods."

Her last period was somewhere back before they crossed the last border. Blanche tried to remember exactly when, but couldn't. There was only this little brown spotting and one morning a brisk flow into the john, and then nothing. It just stopped.

Then, a Sunday morning, she woke with her nightgown soaked and bad cramps.

Willi had medical coverage through his job at the printers, so he posed as husband, and called the *Seguros*. A doctor came, said it looked like a miscarriage and sent her to the Clínica Carvajal.

"But weren't you careful?" Willi asked Carl.

"Of course, she has a diaphragm."

They scraped her out and she slept all Friday. When she woke, she found herself in a long ward between a woman with a large smooth baby and a woman with a small wrinkled one. The family of the woman with the large baby camped all around her, eating out of stackable aluminum pans.

Next day, she felt better, and got up to get a closer look at the babies. *I had a baby in me all that time, this astonishing thing happened to me and I never once believed in it*, she thought. Willi came and held her hand. Carl went out to buy her a raspberry ice.

She tried to ask one of the nursing sisters what the foetus had been.

"*Un muchachito*," she was told, "*de cuatro meses*." She had been four months pregnant, and all the time she thought she was sterile.

Well, it didn't matter. Probably she'd never be able to carry a baby more than four months. Belle had known a woman like that.

Then, a week later, there was the fire.

It must have started under the house where the press corps smoked butts. The wood floor burned through into the room Willi used for a studio. It was on the opposite end from the bedrooms, so they weren't alarmed until the whole side was in flames, and Elsie the dog barking wildly. Willi saved his short wave, a few of his paintings and prints; and Augustina, her trunk. Blanche and Carl saved their clothes and Carl's books. Engines were summoned, and they stood out in the courtyard in front. The press corps danced wildly about, and watched it, all but the walls and grand staircase, burn. Miguelito had been parked across the street, so was saved.

Towards dawn, they drove to the *Pensión* Stein on the Avenida Sexta and slept, the three of them, in one room, without washing their bodies or changing their smoky clothes; they didn't wake until three in the afternoon.

Willi was up first. Carl stirred.

"We can't stay here long, you know," Willi said.

"No, no!" Carl sat up.

"All we need in one of those mud huts," Willi said. "We might build it ourselves."

80

Carl got dressed. "I'll talk to The Doña."

"Of course, you must come to us at Tula," she told Carl, after he told her about the fire and Willi's idea of the mud hut. She sent him out to find Don Rafa at the café.

Don Rafa was in his usual place at the Cafe Mil y Una Noches drinking *café tinto*. Carl told him about the fire.

"How?"

"The press corps," I suspect. "That's what we call the street kids who hang around us. They smoked in the *bodega*."

"You are all safe?"

"Yes, yes."

"Thank God! But the whole, the whole grand pile, left the granite staircase and a couple of walls."

"Cielos!"

"We need something, a shack. It must be cheap."

"Cheap!"

"Yes."

"A mud shack you mean?"

"Yes, and a little land maybe."

"Mud shacks are in continual need of being shored up. That is if they don't wash away entirely in the rainy season, and *animalitos* infest the thatch aside from numerous other…"

"Your wife suggested Tula."

"Ah, you want to be farmers!"

Willi would like it. He thought of all the agricultural advice from Fidel Castro that Willi had taken in over the short wave.

"You will live like peasants."

"We are peasants." Willi, being a Maoist, loved peasants.

"Ah, well now, there is a concrete block hut with a good zinc roof at Las Brumas…"

"It has never been much of a farm, belongs to my wife's family actually. I would have made it pay, but they never cared. There are two outbuildings, and one is empty. There was a caretaker, Don Luciano, occupied it with his son. The son married and we built another for him. Then Luciano moved up the hill to Los Franceses. The son does his work. There is little enough since we hardly go now. There was the accident. I fear Luciano blames himself. In any case, the hut is empty. Plenty of land, plantains, bananas, some chickens, and one cow. There used to be horses. We used to go all the long vacation with the children, the nephews. Then there was the accident. One of my brother's children was thrown from Luciano's mule. It was a sad occasion. My wife took it the hardest, had the mule and horses sold. We've turned to gardening. Perhaps, this year we shall go again. But the hut you are welcome to."

"We would work," Carl insisted.

"But there is Orlando, and his woman helps in the kitchen."

"What is growing there now?"

"Marguerritas, bougainvillea."

"To eat, I mean," said Carl.

"Well, there are chickens, milk."

"Listen, we'll take it," Carl was excited. "But we must work."

"Work, then, *pues*, work." Don Rafa smiled.

82

"Concrete block hut, zinc roof, plenty of land, in the central *cordillera*..." Carl reported back. Blanche was still in bed, drinking iced coffee.

"We'll go!" Willi said.

They gave Elsie the dog to Augustina, and the Renault to Ramos to sell for them; it would never make it over the *cordillera*. The Laundry Magnate who owned the house made a few feeble gestures at blaming them for the fire, but gave it up in the face of their poverty and the testimony of the baker next door that the urchins continually smoked under the house.

At the Casa del Pueblo, they outfitted themselves as cheaply as possible; and the following Thursday, they took a bus to the city to catch a *por puesto* taxi to Tuxpan in the state of Tula.

They left before noon, the taxi soaring along the aerial ribbon that crossed the city, leaving to its own slow pace the fussy old town below, its cafes and verandahs behind bougainvillea vines. Autopista del Este, Autopista del Valle; then, looping westward, onto an older mountain road, and they climbed into the clouds hanging over the city.

A bank of clouds sat on the blue eucalyptus tree tops. A shower hung over the far valley.

It was late afternoon when the clouds lifted and they overlooked the city of Tuxpan. A small metal cross with a hubcap hanging on it marked the spot where a car had gone over the cliff. Then they descended through some small villages of white washed houses with heavy black thatch, a square with a church. Grass bleached colorless.

Only the irrigated cane fields were green here. The surrounding hills were burning, the smoke adding to the heat and dust. A woman in front seat got out with her string bags. The final stop was Tuxpan, a taxi stand in front of the cathedral. They unloaded their duffel bags from the roof. It was near dusk; and since there was no electricity at Las Brumas and Don Rafa advised not arriving at night, they went across the street and reserved two rooms at a dim little hotel with tall spindly wooden pillars holding up an arcade around a patio full of rubber plants.

Tuxpan was a town of three streets of commerce intersected by two broad boulevards. They walked along one of these boulevards, and found a Chinese restaurant; Chinese restaurants here were identical to Chinese restaurants in Chicago, or presumably anywhere. This one was consoling in their homeless state. Will took out the account book and wrote figures on a napkin: They had about ten thousand pesos saved. "It's my opinion," Willi said, "we should spend only on items like clothes, dentists and food we can't grow, like meat, or we could give up meat. There will be eggs and milk."

"We can grow beans, yucca, and tomatoes. We'll each have our jobs: cooking, washing up, washing clothes, plus the cows..."

"Cow," Carl said.

"Yes, and the chickens."

"Have you ever had dealings with chickens?"

"Never, we'll learn. You know," Willi said, "people live here for eight pesos a day. The price of a Coke in a hotel."

"Who told you that?"

"Our washerwoman, I was taking poverty lessons from her. You can live a week on a pound of dried beans, a couple pounds of yucca and rice, a cake of raw sugar, some plantains: That's eighty pesos a week in the city, less in the country.

84

What else do you need?" Willi went on. "A couple pair of cut-offs; you wash them in a stream now and then; dental care, you can't neglect that; the poor don't bother, I know, but I don't agree with that. Reduce things. You need a philosophy of things. What's dispensable, what's not…What was I saying? Oh, fluoride treatments, indispensable and underwear, dispensable. Socks, I admit, have their function, unless you can dispense with shoes. Sandals, an excellent invention, shaving, a waste of time, especially, if you use dispensable blades. Running to the store for dispensable items is dispensable…"

"Go fuck yourself, Willi. I'll shave my frigging legs, if I feel like it," Blanche said.

Next day, they bought tequila, rice, lentils, beans, salt, soap, kerosene, matches, seeds, candles, and took a bus up the mountain just before noon.

Kilómetro Veinticinco was a collection of three or four houses, a small store with a telephone exchange behind. Las Brumas was up the road about a half mile, overlooking the small settlement. They hiked up the hill. Several mud huts crowded against the road, sun-baked and crazed like old China. The road doubled back and Las Brumas came into sight, a wooden house painted white, with a red Eternit roof. The hillside was planted with coffee bushes shaded by plantain trees. Behind the house a pasture sloped steeply up. At the top was a cistern covered with a large concrete slab, and behind that another farmhouse.

Breathless, they stopped to rest. Leaning against the ferrous red gash where the road was carved into the mountainside, they put down the packs and gulped the thin air.

Another turn, and the drive up to the house ran off to the right. The house was surrounded by flowerbeds. *The Doña's work*, Carl thought. The two huts were at the back, off a dirt courtyard, substantial, concrete block structures with zinc roofs. In the doorway of one, a girl stood watching them. Orlando's wife, she was awkwardly built with a large head, probably looked older than she was.

"*Buenas,*" Carl said, and asked for Orlando.

"*Arriba*," she said, pointing up the slope.

Followed by her stare, they looked around. Opposite the huts was a stable with four stalls and a gleaming forage cutter. Coffee beans were spread to dry on the roof and a bougainvillea vine covered the sides. A wash was hung to dry over the vines; another soaked in a bucket.

Their hut was furnished with a wood stove, some pans and dishes, two beds with horsehair mattresses, and an old mahogany wardrobe. On the small front porch were a metal table and chairs.

"Excellent, excellent," Willi kept saying. Nothing but what's necessary. They put away the groceries on two shelves over the stove and unrolled the bedrolls on the two beds. Willi took the back room and Carl and Blanche took the room off the kitchen. Willi started a fire in the stove with some kindling piled on the floor, but found this made the hut unbearably hot. He noticed that the girl had started to cook outside over a small kerosene stove; so, enduring her stares, he fabricated a barbecue with three cement blocks he found around back, and the wood stove's oven rack.

Carl walked up the hill and found Orlando coming down with the red cow and a black dog. He was tall, curly-haired, *mestizo*. "But The Doña isn't here," he kept saying, unable to imagine that any gringo would be visiting in the absence of Doña Luz.

"To help with the work," Carl explained; but this idea seemed unacceptable to Orlando.

"I do the work. Where you from?" he said suddenly in English.

"Chicago."

"I live there," Orlando said.

Where?

"Texas, California. I dream all the time to go back."

Carl laughed.

"Why you come here? There is nothing here," said Orlando.

"Our house we were renting in Las Marias burned. The *Doña* offered us, the hut Luciano's hut. We want to work, you show us…"

Orlando simply stared at Carl. "You hiding out from something?"

"Sort of."

"Ah." This Orlando understood. The cow was pushed into the stable. "I milk her now."

Willi left the fire and followed them in. "This is Willi," Carl said.

"Hiya." Orlando took an aluminum pan from a nail and began filling it. "You can't go back there?"

"We can go back," Willi said. "But we plan to live here."

"Nobody lives here that don't have to." He handed Willi the pan filled with milk. "Take. We don't drink much."

Blanche came in. She had washed her hair under the spigot, and put on shorts. Orlando stared at her and she gave him a frank look. Then he laughed.

Carl inspected the forage cutter's circular blade, oiled and gleaming. Under it was a bin of *caña brava* minced fine. An old saddle hung in the corner.

"Used to be a mule," Orlando said. "One of the Doña's nephews fell off and broke his neck." His eyes kept going to Blanche.

"This is Blanche," Carl said.

"Your woman or his?"

"Mine."

"I was a maintenance man in Texas for some Christian Science people. I take care of a cooling plant. They take care of me, but they don't like me to drink, smoke."

"Your wife should drink milk," Willi said. The girl was pregnant. She stood in the doorway staring at them. Very young; fourteen or fifteen. "When is the baby?"

"January."

There wasn't enough firewood to finish the lentils. Willi moved them to Orlando's stove. They shared some fried plantains and sat around the oil lamp at the metal table drinking Cruz Verde. "We'll get a kerosene stove when we go down to Tuxpan next," Willi said. He was exhausted from his outdoor fire.

The darkness around them was filled with *cigarras* trilling and the mists had begun to descend. The girl, whose name was Miriam, washed up her pans at the spigot in the yard, using the red dust as an abrasive. No one had heard her speak beyond that first word.

"The *Doña* make us marry," Orlando said sheepishly, looking at her.

"A pressure cooker," Willi said. "Cultivating fork, cheese cloth, a colander, garden hose, and sprinkler. I'll try bush beans behind the stable there, and transplant some of that yucca growing wild. Have you had any luck with corn?" he asked Orlando.

"Not much. No rains till December."

"That's what the hose is for?"

"We run water down for few days. Now is dried up."

"No, man, I've looked at that cistern," said Willi. "It only needs cleaning."

He was trying to get Fidel on the short wave saved from the fire; but succeeded only in pulling in a powerful Bonaire gospel station.

The night was cold and damp as the clouds came down. Carl got up twice to close the shutters. Towards dawn, he fell deeply asleep and woke late to the stove going, dispelling the damp and brewing coffee. Carl got up, wrapping himself in a poncho.

The clouds had begun to rise, though some remained caught in the bluish eucalyptus trees of the lower slopes; patches of weak sunlight filtered through. He stood out on the porch and watched Orlando come down from the boundary of The *Doña's* land. Together they pulled the steaming cow out of the stall. Orlando milked her and put her into the near pasture. They minced forage; what they had cut the night before was nearly gone. Carl went behind the stable to where the cane grew and cut down stalks with a machete, while Orlando put them through the hand-operated cutter. When Carl had filled the bin with stalks, he watched Orlando, then took a turn himself at the revolving blade, working until his arms ached.

Orlando went to bed then, after his night of patrolling the boundaries, and the girl, Miriam, came out to resume her silent washing by the pump in the yard.

Willi fried plantains and heated the milk for the coffee; then they walked down to the store below to buy bundles of firewood. The day was warming up and they sat at a wooden table in front of the little store drinking rum in chunky glasses. The storekeeper's wife had left for the market in Tuxpan before dawn and was back with a side of fatback, a beef heart, and some soup bones. These she would retail to the poor shack dwellers around. She agreed to bring them a kerosene stove on her next trip, and sold them some bones and a beef heart.

"We won't come here often," Willi said, but Carl had a feeling they would.

They spent the rest of the morning transplanting the young yucca plants that had gone wild into a plot beside the stable. For lunch, they had more fried plantains and beans. Carl fell asleep after, woke to the smell of Willi's *ocote* fire in the courtyard, bitter in his nostrils. Miriam was cooking too, over the petroleum stove on the porch. He had never been so aware of these processes of food gathering, preparation, and eating.

The late afternoon sun was warm, the air dry and clear. He wandered about the grounds, through vegetable gardens overgrown with *cañabrava* and purple castor, swept and empty stables, plantain grove beside it, then a lean-to chicken house with shelves for roosting, fenced-in yard for scratching. There were some white leghorns with two or three baby chicks, a scrawny rooster. A leather-covered account book hung from a chain. Twenty-four leghorns, purchased 9 February, noted on the flyleaf. Inside were twenty-four columns with daily checks or zeros posted. Most of them seemed to lay daily at the beginning, less now. He went back and counted the chickens: seventeen.

"Leghorns," Orlando said behind him. "Don't lay much anymore, and no good to eat; *muy flacas.*" Carl moved on, through the plantain grove to the side of the big house which overlooked the valley.

The *Doña's* flowers were planted in neat rectangular beds outlined with stones, pebble paths between. *Margaritas*, gardenias, *veranera*, *inmortales*, he recognised; most he couldn't name. When she came, he would ask her. Would she come? He felt her presence in these colorful rectangles, these neat paths.

There was a glassed-in porch on this side of the house, with cement steps painted red. He went up and looked through the panes. There were some blocky red leatherette chairs at one end, a table covered in blue oilcloth, a bookcase with a few creamy paperbacks of the kind The *Doña* sent out to be bound in leather. The door was unlocked, so he went in. He checked a few of the books to see, from the cut and uncut pages, where she had read. The French novels were mostly cut open; of the English titles she had read in their entirety only some essays. Back in Las Marias in her dim library they had been reading Henry Adam's *Mt Saint Michel and Chartres.* He recalled her grave school girl voice:

Over the little church at Fenioux on the Charente, is a conical steeple an infidel might adore.

Always she wanted him to stop her and correct her. Perhaps she will bring the book.

91

He continued around the house. There were rosebushes, a fig tree in green fruit, and a bed of herbs: She had served him an infusion once made with *limoncillo* leaves. It helped the digestion.

The woman from the little store brought them back a kerosene stove next day which greatly simplified cooking and allowed it to be done indoors.

After that, Carl did the errands. He went to the market on the early bus, arriving before seven. At one stall, he bought rice, lentils, and black beans; at another, tomatoes, and corn, which were their staples. Then leaving his basket in the care of a lottery seller, he went to a cafe across the street and had a cup of *tinto* and a *milhojas* pastry, and read one of the books from The *Doña's* library. Afterwards, wandering along Calle Tres de Mayo, he bought little handcrafts: an enamel bowl, a set of pottery cups.

"But why do you buy these things?" Blanche complained, weighing us down. "It isn't as if we'd meant to come just here. To Kilómetro Veinticinco."

"Where, then?" he asked her. She was vexed from the start. Here was no buying *of cinco y seis* tickets to bet on horses, no cantinas that roared with talk. Carl, on the other hand, finding he could sit in the shade under a ceiba tree and cut open the creamy pages of the *Dona's* books here, as well as back in Las Marias, was content.

Willi started painting again in the egg tempera he mixed up himself.

And there was agriculture.

In November, they had their own lettuce, beans, and some yucca. The figs were ripe and Willi put them up in a syrup of *aguapanela*. He learned to make white cheese from the left-over milk, letting it stand three days, then pouring off the whey through a cloth and salting it heavily.

Carl brought back a new white rooster from the market, leading it on a leash. The hens were allowed to roost and six little leghorns were hatched. Carl numbered them and noted their existence in a fresh page of the notebook hanging from the wall.

"I mean it isn't as if we meant to come exactly here," Blanche said from the bed, watching Carl hang up a weaving bought from an Indian claimed to have walked here from La Virginia. A monkey with a triangular green face and a tree. "The monkey is bigger than the tree," said Blanche. Crazy, she was drinking *agave* tea.

"Where is it you want to go then?" he asked.

"How do I know, if we just sit here on this mountain."

Carl sat down on the bed. You oughtn't to drink that stuff.

"It does no harm. Only the *mescal* harms. It makes me feel good, bigger than this mountain. Like that monkey, bigger than the tree. If only we hadn't sold the car, Carl, Carl."

"You want to stay with me?"

"No...yes."

"You'd have left me if we were back there?"

"Maybe, maybe not."

"You're free. We said we'd be free."

"Oh, Carl, Carl."

"What do you want? What?"

"Hold me."

"You shouldn't..."

"Hold me!" She was naked, perspiring. They rocked together. "I want..."

"What? What?"

"Help me, Carl, help me. I'm disappearing." They lay together, perspiring.

"What do you do with your old lady?" she whispered.

"Nothing, talk."

"What do you talk about?"

"Churches."

"Churches. Oh, hold me hold me, don't move…Yes, yes, it's a nice monkey. His face is green and he's bigger than the tree. Tell me, tell me about churches. What church do you talk about?"

"Chartres. It has two towers, built in different centuries. The older one is finer."

"Why?"

"It solves the problem of changing from a square to a hexagon."

"Ah, is that what The *Doña* worries about?"

"She's a good woman."

"Am I good?"

"Yes. I wish you could be happy."

"I can't, Carl; that's what I'm trying to tell you."

"Why, why?"

"It's death. I feel death here."

"What death?"

"That child that fell off the horse. I don't know…the hens. Death, Carl."

"I don't understand. An accident, a couple hens…"

"It's here. It's why they don't come."

"They'll come."

"Your old lady talks about churches. That's funny. She's old, Carl…"

"Not so old, younger than him."

94

"Forty at least, She can't have children."

"She's good, good."

"How, good, how?"

"…takes care of us all. Orlando, Miriam, the gardens, the nephews, and us."

"Old, Carl. They're thousands of years older than we are. Don't you feel it?"

"Maybe."

"You like it. You like to read her old books. But you don't see. It's death."

"She brings up his brother's children," he said. "They have nothing. She sends them to good schools."

"And Don Rafa brings up the children of the *telegrafista* down in the village."

"Who says that?"

"Everyone knows they're his." She held out the cup to him. "Drink."

He sipped the musty tasting infusion. Felt nothing. Like Willi, he preferred Cruz Verde.

Each day was sunny as the previous one. It was the *verano*. The pastures were brown, and above *Los Franceses,* fires blackened the mountain. One of Carl's young reds died, and three more of the old leghorns.

But, at the end of November, the big house was opened up. The daughter of the *Telegrafista* came up to cook and Orlando's wife moved over to help in the kitchen. A week later, The *Doña* arrived with *Doña* Bertha and the four nephews, who slept in the bunk beds in the annex to the house. They would stay through Christmas.

Three large meals were prepared daily. Occasionally, when the kitchen in the big house became too hot, dishes were baked in Orlando's oven and carried over to the house. Sometimes, the remains of a meal, a *flan*, or a dish of baked plantains would be sent out to them.

The *Doña's* English lessons resumed at ten every morning. They met on the glass-enclosed porch at the back of the house overlooking the garden with the gravel paths.

"Have you everything you need?" she asked him in her careful English on the first day.

"Oh, yes. The woman at the *abasto* brings us supplies from Tuxpan, and I go once a week."

"You must go with Juan, while we are here."

"Thank you."

"They charge too much, at the *abasto*. I know you have limited…and I wish to pay you the hundred pesos weekly for the lessons."

"But it is too much," he said, "we are living here without paying."

"No, no, I wish to pay."

"You are very kind."

Orlando's woman brought a tray with *café tinto* and some white rolls. She stared at Carl, unable to comprehend that someone who cleaned out the hen house was also received here in the big house and served by herself.

"The little boys come here to recover their health on the vacation. The air of the mountains opens the appetite. We do not have the change of season, so the body suffers unless one changes the altitude."

"It is very beautiful here."

"Yes, when it suns."

"When the sun shines," he corrected her.

"When the sun shines as now, there is nowhere more beautiful. When it rains, it is a sad climate some say."

"And you?"

"It is my home. My family is of Tuxpan. It is pleasing to me, the high, the cold, the black pines, the white washed houses…"

He watched her face. It was pale as usual, but animated. She had been wearing black since she arrived. It seemed that a cousin had died, and the women in the family had adopted *luto*. The black had shocked him when she first arrived, and made her look haggard, but today, she had thrown a blue sweater over her shoulders and was wearing a pair of slacks for the country. He told her she looked well.

"The place where one is from, where one has been happy," she said. "It is a climate for serious men they say. My grandfather wore always a black hat and a cloak. He could recite all of Robledo by heart."

"And why did you leave?"

"I marry. Don Rafa dislikes here. He has arguments with the priests at the seminary where they sent him."

"But it must bore you."

She turned her fine eyes on him, "A woman's life."

"No, no, why ever?" He cried, embarrassing her.

"The cow does well," she said, turning the subject.

"Yes, yes."

"She is old, but she does well, yes; when we are living in the city, drinking the milk from the store that one never knows what they put in it, I say to Don Rafa, What a grateful thing it is to come here and drink the milk of a cow that is…how do you say, *una vaca conocida*?"

"A cow one is acquainted with."

"Yes, yes," she laughed. A cow one is acquainted with. She looked him timidly in the face. "You will go back to your country one day, I am sure."

"No, no, never to that."

"That what?"

"That waiting to begin. Nothing could begin."

"But one's county!" she said.

"One's county…one's county drops bombs where there is nothing to bomb. Everyone knows it is a disgrace, and yet it has gone so far it cannot be stopped, or anyone say it's been for nothing."

"Still, it will be over one day. You will go back."

"I cannot for now, in any case."

"I cannot understand it," she said, "To have such a dislike for one's country. We criticise ourselves all the time, as you notice…my husband yet we always love…"

One of her small nephews had come into the room.

"I am afraid it is a custom here," she said, caressing the child, "for sons of wealthy families to buy…how shall I say? To pay a sum to avoid the conscription."

"I could have done that," Carl said. "That is, I could have stayed…in school; but I'm glad I didn't. It is better, as Willi says, to reject, to make one's life a statement."

"I do not understand, I'm afraid," she said. The child leaned heavily against her, pressing for her attention. "How can one reject one's entire…that is to say…one's life?"

"Do you despise me?"

"Despise you? But hardly know you," she said, innocent of how she injured him.

Doña Berta came in and called him to her. "He is no trouble," said Doña Luz, allowing the child to slip from her

98

lap. Berta, who had eight children, was a small woman with a narrow dark face. She was married to a brother of Don Rafa's who was relatively poor. At eleven every morning, she played hearts on the verandah with *misia* Eulalia and her daughter from up the hill.

"I don't know," Carl said. "I can't explain it, but my first *positive* feeling in these past four or five years has been deciding to come here…" He felt slightly off balance, having been interrupted by the child's mother as he was about to tell her more…the waiting, the impossibility of beginning a life when everything depended on a draft number, but, as she had said, she barely knew him.

"But," she said to Carl, "you have ruin your career, your life. What is there for you here?"

"This place, useful work."

"I'm afraid it is not a…how you say…a serious farm. The soil is poor. It is for the air we come, the flowers…" She moved a gray porcelain dove to a high shelf out of reach of the child. "Still, your mother, she is sad. It is such a distance. I mean, to live in a foreign country."

"You learn a foreign language," he said.

"Ah, but it is only to travel as a tourist, to read, perhaps. You think it is useless, that I should rather play hearts with the others?"

"No, no! I admire you. You are altogether admirable!"

"An idle woman."

"No, you must read! And you might travel; but you said you never would again."

"Never as I once did."

"How is that?"

"Young and alone." She laughed.

"What is funny?"

"It is an old family joke. An old aunt, very rich, she never left Envigado. They had a farm there, a very old-fashioned family. One year her husband made great preparations, took a train at La Victoria and a ship at Los Olmos, and went to Europe. My aunt stayed in Envigado and crocheted her tablecloths and played games of *tute* and drank her chocolate at eleven. She sighed when she thought of her husband. 'The poor man, alone in Paris,' she would say."

"Ah, yes, yes!" He laughed. How charming she was when she told these stories.

"Alone in Paris, ah yes. Will you have a biscuit?"

"Thank you."

"It is a terrible thing, the bombing. You are not mistaken, I hope," she said.

"It is to be heard every evening on the radio."

"Ah, then I suppose it must be true, the radio." She turned her gray eyes on him, charming woman. *What had produced her? What slow education, what long breeding produced these reticences, these occasional drolleries, this deep gaze?*

Blanche washed the way Miriam did, soaping the clothes with a green naptha bar and spreading them on the grassy verge of the courtyard to bleach; then holding them under the spigot and stretching them over the *veranera* vines to dry. They often washed together, but the girl never spoke. *If I had a child in me, I'd be the same, like a bitch in the sun*, Blanche thought.

After the washing the clothes, she washed her hair and shaved her legs. Carl brought her blades despite Willi's desire to let all hair grow. She let her armpits sprout, but not her legs. Then, with a sprig of *veranera*, she cleaned under her toenails,

100

between her teeth, into her ears, around her clitoris, sniffing herself with pleasure. A dun-colored iguana watched her. She was hidden from curious eyes by the *veranera*, but she didn't care who looked at her. The burning *ocote* reminded her of autumn. Here there was no autumn. Only some weather the winds brought over the mountain.

Nearby, Willi worked dung into the soil and set out his tomato and pepper seedlings. The seeds Luciano gave him had begun to sprout: Amaranth, ancient food of the Aztecs. He planned to upgrade the fodder with it, use leaves and beans in soup. It was a nearly forgotten food according to Luciano. Willi had written his father to research it.

He noted the rain clouds hung over the *cordillera*. *Let them come soon*, he thought, *sprinkling the seedlings*. Just past noon, he used the new shit hole behind the plantains, covered his contribution to the collection of night soil with loose clay. It was preferable to the smelly latrine. After, he took a shower in the stall behind the stable, washing his cut-offs and his t-shirt at the same time. The red clay stains didn't come out completely. He hung the clothes over the wall of the shower stall to dry and pulled on a clean shirt and a clean pair of cut-offs hanging there. They were stiff and scratchy and the pockets had fallen off, but serviceable. He passed Blanche, behind the *veranera*, smoking. She handed him her little clay pipe. It was rather good stuff, bought in the Café Media Luna from an old *marijuanero*.

"You never paint me anymore."

"I'll paint you now." He went to the hut for his pad.

"Shall I take off my things?"

"No."

"Why? I always used to in Las Marias."

"All right, may as well get all the joints and muscles."

She stepped out of her shorts and pulled off her jersey. "Is that all you get?"

"Frankly, no."

"Is that true, Willi?"

"I feel like any other man."

"Then why don't you want me?"

"I control myself."

"Why bother?"

"Like Gandhi, I use the energy for other things."

"Did he draw naked women?"

"He took young women in his bed and never touched them."

"Stuff!"

"Truth."

"How do you want me?"

"Bend your left knee and raise yourself on your elbow."

"What if they touched him?" She asked after a silence.

"Who?"

"Gandhi. What if the women touched him?"

He didn't say. "Put your arm across your belly."

"Like this?"

"Yeah. Relax it more; spread your fingers."

She had relaxed. Her head had drooped. They were both buzzed from the pipe.

He had outlined the head, drooping against a knee. Her uncut hair covered her breasts. One leg had been extended, and her long prehensile toes dominated the foreground. In the background, the brown plantain leaves had drooped against the ringed trunks. Their greener leaves had shaded the glossy coffee bushes. Above the plantains, there had been pasture where the Cow One Knows grazed just below the fires. Its eye had reflected the fires, and the enamel blue sky.

He went back to the drooping head. His own head had cleared.

Willi won't touch this beautiful woman, but he had seen Carl walking in the garden with The *Doña*. He had seen Orlando owning her with his eyes, had wakened in the night to hear her getting up and whispering to him on the stoop as he paused in his nightly rounds of the property.

It was nearly noon. Carl had been cooking a chicken on the petroleum stove on the porch of their hut.

"I'm hungry," Blanche said, and unfolded herself, and picks up her clothes.

Willi was sweating. He stood back and looked at his painting. He didn't know how he had achieved it, but there it was, the sadness of Carl's woman, caught among the banana leaves.

Carl met Sonia and Sergio first when he accompanied Luz on her rounds of Catholic charity, distributing baskets of eggs, and preserves in the neighborhood. A teacher and two children sitting in a neat little cottage, served them coffee, warned them about a coming truckers' strike. This was Sonia. Her husband Sergio was out with the strikers. Unlike the other houses they visited, this house had no oleograph of the Sacred Heart on the wall, Machetes rather. They were Marxists, exiles from over the border.

Carl brought Willi to meet them. They rode up on the afternoon bus.

"This woman is a teacher, you say?" Willi asked. He was excited.

"Yes."

It's your intellectual proletariat. Teachers here, I'm told, only make menial wage. Their only resource is revolution.

"And they have some crops."

"Yes. The coffee crop looked to be farther along than ours."

"So, it is all here…The Maoist elements. The agricultural base. The political awareness."

Willi's excitement reminded Carl of Carl Marx's frustrated desire to encounter a genuine German Socialist.

He watched out the window of the bus for the nearest stop where they could get out and walk up the hill to the farm. As he remembered it was just beyond Kilómetro Treinta where Juan had turned off and headed up a rutted road as far as the Mercedes would go. Yes, here was the little crossroads, with the pharmacy and the telephone exchange with the little *abasto* even smaller than their own little village.

They found Sergio at home that day, sorting coffee beans with his son. Sonia gripped Carl's hand and smiled. "He is home today, you see. I'm always afraid of the day he won't come home."

Sergio got a bottle of Ron Viejo from the kitchen and brought it out to the table on the front porch. He was a square, sturdy man like his wife, his smooth, beardless face reddened over the cheekbones by the altitude.

"So, you stay with *Don* Rafa, eh? I have met him, one of the old Liberals and one of the Great Talkers. They couldn't even kill El Cóndor," said Sergio.

"The mountain will defeat the plain. Here in the *cordillera* is our future, our party, our leaders. The city cannot corrupt them. We wait. But we prepare…"

"Listen, listen, I will show you." Sergio got up and led them through a small back room and out through the dusty back yard, up the hill Carl had climbed before. He parted a thicket of vine, pulled: away a pallet of weathered boards over which a mesh of pine branches had been stapled. Behind, a tunnel had been dug into the red clay.

Sergio pulled out a crate and pried it open. It was filled with rifles wrapped in rags.

"M-14s," he said, unwrapping the greasy cloth. "Fires 7.62 millimeter cartridges; has a range up to seven hundred meters. And this?" He dug out another. "Grenade launcher. Aluminium barrel, has a range between a hand grenade and a mortar."

He pulled out another crate and unwrapped a pair of machine guns. "M-16s, modified for automatic fire."

"Where do you get them?" Willi asked.

"The AKM's come in the powdered milk."

"What?"

"The *Centros Rurales* receive aid shipments. I tell you this because you are exiles like us?"

"Yes, yes," Willi said.

"I take the risk of trusting you, right?"

"Yes, yes."

"The rice and the milk are sent in from Eastern Europe, then they are distributed by the *Rurales.* These weapons, are hidden in caves in thirty-four districts. We avoid concentrations of weapons, same as we avoid troop concentrations, disseminated focus. We go on with our lives, but there are periods of training. We have seventeen *focos.* We are the closest to the city. It is, here, most dangerous to operate."

105

"Some weapons come also from the *cuartel*," Sergio said, rewrapping the machine guns in rags. "Sabotage, desertions take place. We surrounded a company on manoeuvres a month ago, took over a hundred M-16s. Since then, we've had to be very careful." He pushed away the crate of weapons, pulled out a cardboard box, "My books."

Carl knelt to look. There was *The Marx Engels Reader,* Debray, a quarto edition of Zola's *Germinal* on creamy paper like the *Doña's* books.

"I must hide them now. It becomes more dangerous." Sergio pushed the boxes back in and straightened up. "You were right to leave there," he said. "It is because of that that I show you this. It is all one struggle, yes?"

They walked back down the hill. "You say nothing, especially to D*on* Rafa. He is a good man. He was in prison in the days of Salazar they say. It is only, he talks, and the time for that is over. 'The urge to destroy is also the creative urge,' Bakunin said. The Liberal's parliamentary democracy is nothing but a fraud which the upper class uses to dominate the masses. These gentlemen we have now in the Palacio de Armas will perpetuate themselves until the devil knows."

They sat under a silk cotton tree with the bottle of Ron Viejo.

"Our other weapon is the strikes. But this, we must leave mostly to our brothers in the city. At the end, though, at the end, we will all come together as it was in Petrograd. It must ripen."

"You have a good soil here," Willi said, nudging at an ant hill with his sandal.

"Yes, volcanic ash. Better than over your way. Life is good. My children grow; my wife has her profession; but one lives for ideas or one is a brute."

"Ach! Ideas!" cried Sonia, who stooped nearby, sorting coffee beans.

"For justice, *mi amor*," he said.

She bent over her beans, not answering.

The bruised clouds remained just behind the mountains and the rains didn't come, but the Virgin remained, untouched. "Run, see, Olga," Berta said every afternoon at cards.

"See if she's still there."

"Still up there, eh, turning the heads of kitchen girls," said Rafa, sitting on their stoop. "You get this talk of miracles when a religion is new and when it's in decay. A compound in putrefaction gives up its elements. It's simple chemistry. It all begins in miracles and goes out in miracles." Carl sat staring up at the fires. Willi sucked a lime.

"But who's to do something!" Carl erupted.

"Yes, years, we talked, I admit. Precious little we did. My wife distributes her baskets; I suppose that's something. But it's never going to end the misery of this mountain."

"Trouble is," said Willi, "no one's seen what could be made of it."

"Of what?" Don Rafa asked. "*La miseria*? What can be made of it but more misery…?"

"No, no, limits, possessing only what's necessary. Where do the diminishing returns begin in possessing? Knowing that," Willi insisted.

"Ah, well, asceticism. It's an elite understands such things."

"You give money to one of these *miserables*. Does he spend it on wholesome food or necessities? No, he shows off with a banquet, spends it all on drink and *bizcochos*," said Rafa.

"Maybe the fault lies in the money," Willi said.

"How so?"

"Money creates diffuse desires, unreality," Willi said.

"But can we to do away with it? It's there and everyone wants it," Carl asked.

"By faith."

"Faith in what?"

"In this lime," Willi said, holding one up. "In its reality, it's nourishment, its beauty. There's no use hoarding it; it will spoil."

"And who's to be prophet of this faith?"

"Its prophet will come. For every truth, there's never lacked a prophet."

"You're right about faith of course," said Rafa. "Nothing's ever accomplished without passion. We're an age short of passion, of symbol; whatever's up there…Virgin, well she's dying; Pisanista flag, well they lost in '59. I carried their banner through the streets once myself. Pisano inspired a certain…an honest man, you know, you had to call him that. Bad stammer. Poignant that he'd stand up in public at all, put himself forward, decades of mass murder in the countryside. Liberals, Conservatives slitting each other's throats. He'd open the jails. 'The forgiving has to start somewhere,' he said, barely able to spit the words out. You had to admire. He lost in '61. In 65, he made the mistake of accepting communist support, and lost even the nomination."

Then, one night the rains came. Willi heard the drumming on the zinc roof and thought of the cistern filling, of the pigs having their baths again and becoming sleek.

The mountains turned green again in a matter of hours it seemed. The Virgin was saved, supposedly, but they all stopped looking up at her, and one day she wasn't there anymore.

On a day in the second week of December, just after the morning storm, one of the children of the storekeeper below came up with a message from Sonia: would *Don* Will and *Don* Carl come to her at the *abasto* without saying anything to anyone? They walked down the hill and found her alone in the little room behind the store.

"You will come with me and talk to him, please, *un Norteamericano.* They have kidnapped him and brought him to us," she said.

"What? Who?"

"Our people in the city, rich *norteamericano,* he is a vice-president of a company. He is sick, dying maybe. It seems he wishes to die. You must talk to him. We cannot. He does not understand. You will see. There is a bus in an hour. You will return with me, and come back on the morning bus?"

"Yes, yes, of course," Willi said.

They sat and drank *aguardiente* in the chilly back room. There was a bus at eleven o'clock.

"We learned from the newspapers he is a diabetic," Sonia went on. "We have sent for insulin, a doctor. He has been in the *cordillera* for three weeks without insulin. It was too far. There were no doctors, so they brought him secretly to us. He is very weak; we must hurry. They are asking a quarter of a million dollars for his return. Our liaison says they are willing

109

to pay. He is a vice-president, as I told you. The negotiations are going forward, but we must keep him alive."

"But what must we say to him?" Carl asked.

"That he must let the doctor examine him, test his urine, let us give him the injections, that his company wishes to pay the money."

"Always, before we have returned these men alive. It is because of this they pay our ransoms."

The bus came. Sonia leaned close to speak in whispers: "It has never been our experience they die for their companies; you know. We don't know what the matter with him is. The doctor is risking much to come, but he is one of us."

They had given Paul Seybolt their bedroom. He lay on the cheap chenille spread, wearing chinos and a dirty tennis shirt. Willi sat on a bench at the far end of the little room. Carl stood in the doorway with Sonia.

"We speak English," Willi said.

The man said nothing.

Willi moved closer: "Why won't you let a doctor see you?"

"Good God!" laughed the man. "What next?"

"You're a diabetic?" Carl asked.

"So, you've been reading about me in the newspapers."

"We know they wish to return you alive, that things are going forward. Your company wishes to…"

"Who, precisely, are you?" Paul Seybolt said, looking at Carl.

"No one, really," Carl shrugged.

"What are you doing in this place?"

"A little of this and that," Willi said. "That's not the point."

"Ah, yes, 'No one really,' 'A little of this and that.' I have a son wants to be no one really. Sleep therapy, they're trying."

Seybolt lay with his eyes closed. He seemed to have exhausted himself. When he began speaking again had to come close to the bed.

"I was co-founder of this company they're demanding quarter of a million from; did the newspapers say that?"

"I don't know," Carl said. "We didn't see the papers."

"He will not eat," Sonia said. "He hasn't eaten for two days." There was perspiration odor in the room, foot odor.

"Fourteen-hour days we used to put in." Paul Seybolt found the strength to say. "I was worth a couple million then...Then, the big time. When we first came down here, company put us up in the Tucuman-Sheraton for four months while my wife searched for a house had enough style for us. You think that didn't cost...?"

"You're depressed," Willi said.

"Yes, depressed. Do you blame me? Let me finish. Even then, I was worth something to us. Then I had a heart attack; my son was put to sleep for three weeks to cure his maladjustment. We were in the hands of doctors, pills to sleep and pills to wake up. Then my wife left me. I live alone in a twenty-room house. Diminishing returns..."

"Your company wishes to pay."

"In the hands of doctors." The voice was weakening.

"Listen, man, they want to return you alive!" Willi shouted.

"They have their wants and I have mine," said Paul Seybolt, falling back on the pillow.

111

"You want to die?" Willi asked.

"Probably I do, yes." Seybolt took a couple deep breaths, then said, "Tell me, are you one of these?"

"We are friends," Willi said.

"Ah, friends. Yes. Yes, probably I will die. They chose the wrong man, tell them."

Carl went in the kitchen where Sergio was. "Can you have the injections given forcibly?"

"Perhaps, the pharmacist gave me a kit to test the urine."

"How soon can the money be found?"

"They are still negotiating."

They sat at the kitchen table and had meat pies with hot chocolate. The rain continued. "I think there is more to treating him than just insulin," Sonia said. "I think there are matters about diet. He asks for *aguardiente* but will not eat."

Sonia cleared the table and set out a bottle of rum. The children worked on geometry problems at the foot of the table under the oil lamp. At about nine-thirty, the doctor came: a frightened man in his sixties. He had been contacted by telegram and had never before in his life received a telegram, he told them.

"Have you brought the insulin?" Sonia asked, serving him a cup of chocolate.

"Yes. I could hardly decipher the message. I was so flustered. Have you the urine? They told me they gave you a kit."

"Yes." Sonia brought the urine in a preserve jar. The doctor dipped a tape in it:

"You must do this twice a day. If the green patch turns brown, as you see here, increase the insulin injections. Then, this pink patch…if it darkens, there is a ketosis. You must give extra feedings. Who is to give the injection?"

"I," said Sonia.

"We can begin with forty units in the morning. If the patch turns brown, give another twenty in the evening." He mopped the sweat off his face. "I sincerely doubt you can handle this."

"We must handle it," said Sonia.

"He's four plus," the doctor said, comparing the little tab to a chart on the side of the bottle, "But no ketosis so far. Simply giving insulin is not the entire solution. You have insulin shock to avoid. He becomes weak and perspires, you must give sugar water and hold the injection."

"Yes, yes, I understand," Sonia said.

They went in the bedroom and held him down while the doctor observed Sonia give the injection. It was easy; there was no strength in him. The doctor examined his eyes and feet. There was an infected toenail. "That's bad. Use this Betadine solution I'll leave you."

They went back in the kitchen and Sonia offered the doctor an *empanada*. He waved it away. His stomach had been upset all day.

"A little cup of *manzanilla*?" Sonia offered.

"No, this is serious, serious. It will have to be hurried up."

"There is nothing we can do," Sergio said. "It is a matter of currency. The money must be usable."

"Yes, yes, well I've done what I can do."

He picked up his bag. "Cannot come back, it is too dangerous."

The captive dozed.

"Perhaps it will be all right, if only he will eat. As long as he is so weak, we can handle the injections and the urine,"

113

Sonia said. "You must go now. No one must know. If we need you, I will send to the *abasto*."

They went back on the bus. No one had noticed their absence.

On Wednesday, Willi went up. Seybolt looked thinner. His face was shiny with perspiration. "He will not eat," Sergio said.

"Sometimes, when he wants the aguardiente very badly I can get him to eat a little soup before I let him drink," Sonia said.

"But it is not enough," said Sergio. "I called the doctor; he will send someone from the *Rurales* to put a nose tube."

"Tell him," Sonia said, "he will save himself the tubes if he will eat. You can tell him he will be tied down and very uncomfortable."

"I know, I know," said Seybolt, understanding her. "Let them do what they must. I'm too weak to fight them."

"The money is arranged," Sergio said. "It is only to take him to the meeting place. But it is far and he will not stand the trip as he is. We cannot show them a corpse."

"Why do you do this?" Willi said to the man on the bed. "Your disease can be controlled."

"My disease, yes. Try it yourself. I have the childhood type even though it started when I was thirty. You want to see the muscles in my legs?" He pulled up his pant leg. The thigh muscle was pulled up in a knot, as if no longer attached to the tendon and bone.

"Impotent too; you never knew that, did you, about diabetes? You think it's just a matter of a little insulin."

They brought the lentil soup that Sonia had on the stove, but he shook his head. Sergio gave him some guava juice with the aguardiente in it. "It will do him harm in the long run, but maybe in the short…"

Sergio poured them all a drink.

"So, you do a little 'this and that'?" Seybolt said, looking a little revived.

"Yes; we farm a little," Willi said.

"What do you grow?"

"Pepper, beans, and corn."

Seybolt sat up. "Have to pee."

They helped him up. He stood weakly, with Willi's help, and urinated into a pail in the corner. Sonia dipped one of the tapes in the urine. Negative. She frowned. There was a slight ketosis. Seybolt started to fall coming back to the bed. Will caught him, helped him zip up his fly.

"They pee like any other *miserable*," said Sergio, "these vice presidents."

The afternoon rain had begun. Sonia put bowls under two leaks. A man in a poncho came to the door. Sergio went out in the yard to talk to him.

"We have the Jeep," Sergio said to Sonia when he came back in. "We start next Monday. They will send someone this afternoon with the nose tube and the Similac. Tell him this," Sergio said to Carl, "and ask him once more if he will eat."

Willi shook Seybolt awake and explained about the nose tube. The man's skin felt loose on his bones, "Give me more *aguardiente*."

They gave him the *aguardiente* in milk this time, and he spat it out.

They waited, drinking Cruz Verde now. Seybolt slept, perspiring in spite of the chill. The rain stopped and the sun shone briefly in through the shutters, then it was dark. They put off eating. "He must be here soon," Sergio said. "Or I will have to go."

A boy of sixteen or so finally came at nearly six-thirty with a nose tube and three cans of Similac.

"And the student?" Sonia asked.

"He's been arrested."

"But why? He's done nothing…?"

"It will be as an example," said Sergio. "They know whoever has the gringo will be looking for medical help. The student attended meetings."

"Do you know how to insert the tube?" Sonia asked the boy hopelessly.

"I know nothing."

Sergio was taking down his poncho from the nail. He would go for the midwife in the next village.

"Go, *mijo*," Sonia said. "He is dying. I feel it."

The schoolbooks were pushed to one end of the table, and they sat down in the kitchen and had the soup and fried plantains. "Perhaps, it's lucky they arrested him," Sonia said. "They might have let him lead them to us."

"Pig!" Willi jumped up and stood in the bedroom door: "Pig!" he shouted at the sleeping man. "You'll let these people be your murderers!"

Seybolt opened his eyes.

"These are good, decent people. They don't want you to die!"

Seybolt wiped his face on the sheet. "Give me *aguardiente*."

"No, *aguardiente*! Soup. You will drink soup! Bring it!" He gestured to Sonia. She brought a cup of the thick broth.

116

"Good people, and you will destroy them!" Willi shouted. Sonia handed him the cup. "Drink, now!" He held the cup to the sick man. "Drink!"

Seybolt drank and gagged.

"Drink!" Willi yelled. But Seybolt pushed the cup away. "Tube down your nose, you want that?"

Seybolt lay on the bed, weakened and gasping; but shaking his head, "No, no…!" They left him and went back in the kitchen. *Our nerves are giving out*, Willi thought. He'd better come, he'd better come soon.

They sat, silent, listening.to the beetles bump against the shutters. A parade of them came in under the door and crossed the room and went out again under the back door. "We built in their path," Sonia said. "Now they come through any way they can or knock themselves dead trying. Every morning, I sweep them up."

After they had finished eating, Sonia and the girl washed up the dishes. The boy sat at the; table cleaning the chimneys of the oil lamps. "You should be in bed," Sonia said without her usual conviction, so they stayed up.

"These will be different," Sonia said after a while. "These will be a doctor and an engineer."

"Ay, mami, ya no!"

"Yes, the boy a doctor, the girl an engineer. It is decided. They are excellent students. They will have scholarships if God pleases."

"They are each top in their examinations. They will go to the technical school at Los Olmos and to the *Nacional*. Those

117

who finish in the top three at the technical are given full scholarships."

"*Ya basta Mami!*"

"Listen, Don Willi. You two be quiet! You two have nothing to do with this! If anything happens next week…"

"*Que va a pasar, Mami!*"
"The *Doña,* go to The *Doña.* They are innocent children. She will understand that."

"Yes, yes, of course," Willi said.

"My brother's address…here, here!" She pulled a trunk out from under a daybed in the corner of the kitchen, opened it and took out a leatherette box which contained a stack of letters. 'Here'. Taking a blank envelope, she wrote two addresses. "My brother, who lives in Pellicer, and my sister-in-law in the capital. The *Doña* will see they are sent to one or the other."

"Of course, of course."

"I have told them to run to the cave up there and hide. They will wait for you there."

"Yes, yes."

"A doctor and an engineer, you will remember."

Sergio came back alone at about eight thirty.

"She would not come!" Sergio said. "She demonstrated to me its use."

They sat the gringo up and tied his hands behind his back. Sonia sat on his legs and Willi grasped him around the chest. Sergio held the tube up to the light of the oil lamp hung over the bed and blew up a little balloon at the end.

118

"If he would swallow it, it would be simple; but since he certainly won't, it must be inserted through the nose. Miller-Abbot tube," he murmured with satisfaction, applying Vaseline and deflating the bulb at the end. "The little balloon is blown up when the thing is in place and the intestine moves it along. Hold him now."

Paul Seybolt shook his head violently, but Willi grasped it.

"Oopa, it's in!" Sergio said, threading it rapidly down, noting the gradations. Then it stopped.

"Not far enough," Sergio frowned. "This mark must pass the nostril."

Paul Seybolt had become very still.

"He's closing off the gullet. I can feel it." Sergio pulled out the tube.

"Give him *aguardiente*," Willi said. They held the glass to his lips. He retched, drank.

"Let him rest a bit." Sergio wiped his face on his sleeve.

"He's very drunk," Sonia said. "I don't like his color. Try again."

They sat him up again. He was almost dead weight this time. The tube went down. "If only, we haven't killed him with *aguardiente*." Sonia got the Similac and attached a funnel to the end of the tube. While Sergio held it up, she poured the gruel in.

"Is it going down?"

"Maybe, you've made it too thick."

"I followed the directions on the can."

"There, there it goes. He held the tube higher."

"Something to hold it; I can't much longer," Sergio said.

"The mosquito net, tie it to the…"

119

That worked well. Sergio gave the funnel to Willi and found some rubber bands, taking his belt, he hung the buckle off the hook; and then, with the rubber bands, he fastened the funnel to the lower end of the belt.

Sonia stood on a chair to fill the funnel every few minutes or so. "It goes faster now," she said. Paul Seybolt was asleep and snoring, but his color seemed better.

"I thought we were lost. Maybe we are lost. He'll revive. But will we get him to Las Cruces? It's six hours by Jeep," Sergio said.

"It made me itch to 'throw down my shovel and go out there and shoulder a rifle with Chu Teh,'" Willi told Carl when he got back.

"What?" said Carl.

"You won't guess who said that."

"Who?"

"Uncle Joe Stilwell. After Chiang sent him home, just before the whole Nationalist façade came down to the tune of billions invested. One of these remarks almost got him in trouble with McCarthy."

"Who was Chu Teh?"

"One of Mao's guys, Uncle Joe was one of my dad's heroes, Vinegar Joe. He loved the Chinese soldier, saw how the Communists cared for their own. He even went up there and saw them. Big, healthy guys, trained, cared for. And he saw how Chiang never even noticed things like his people were starving, soldiers left to die on the field, while he worried about a shipment of watermelons."

"Agrarian reformers," Uncle Joe called them.

"Sonia asked me to have these people here help the children if anything happens. But, better wait to see if it's necessary."

In the big house, they prepared *Nochebuena.* The *Doña* gathered moss, brought out the bark stable, the porcelain holy family—the Child and the Magi left hidden in excelsior until the last. On the day of the *Iluminación,* the first of the nine candles was lit and family, servants, the three gringos gathered before The *Doña's* nativity scene, which took up a whole end of the verandah; a sandy plain with little oases made of real plants and moss.

And each night, The *Doña* read one of the nine prayers: *"Bendita eres entre mujeres, Y bendito el fruto…"* while *Don* Rafa smoked in the courtyard set off *estrellitas,* little sticks of gunpowder, tossing them in a high arc over the plantains. Eight days, seven days; the porcelain kings began their journey over the mossy plain. The beasts waited, stolid, and Orlando's wife, too, waited heavily on her knees:

"Bendita eres entre mujeres y bendito el fruto de tu vientre, Jesús."

Berta's husband came from the city. He was a quiet man. When the children bothered him, he went out to hoe in the garden.

"Another Christmas," *Don* Rafa remarked to Carl one day in Tuxpan. "How time goes. As Ortega y Gasset said somewhere, 'If life were a toothache that would be an advantage.'"

Carl had finished his grocery shopping and Rafa had replenished his little supply of fireworks, so they walked together to the Café Media Luna. It would rain any minute.

Don Rafa ordered two glasses of rum.

"Oh, by the way, there are things known about them up there, your friends," he said.

"Who?"

"Sergio Molina and his wife. Evidently they are connected with the holding of a wealthy industrialist."

"How did you know?"

"Why in *El Mundo* of course."

"*El Mundo!*" It hadn't occurred to Carl any of the matters they had witnessed those two rainy afternoons up on the mountain could find their way into a newspaper.

But of course, they would. Seybolt's kidnapping had been news for weeks before they met him. How could they have been so stupid not to watch the papers! How could they have simply gone back to their chores and expected to one day go up there and find Sonia and Sergio back at their coffee beans and the children at their geometry…!

"They are among a group of suspects. What do you know for a fact?"

"Well, nothing, Sergio organizes strikes. That's all we know. Your wife also knows that." *Should he perhaps confide in this man*, Carl wondered. Could he help? He noted Rafa giving a slow survey of a young woman sitting at a table nearby and decided not.

"It is said the poor wretch is presumed to be half dead with sugar, and that he is hidden somewhere around here."

"Of that we heard nothing. Willi likes to go up there and talk about the soil with Sergio."

The mangoes ripened and the margaritas bloomed extravagantly; the garden in riot after the rains.

The fourth night before *Nochebuena* the pregnant child knelt heavily in the candlelight, and Olga from the kitchen sang a barbarous carol from Chocotán accompanied by the nephews banging pan lids. *Don* Rafa shared a bottle of Cruz Verde with Luciano. They set off two *volcanes,* which sputtered down the hillside into the cane.

A bat woke Blanche at four. She heard Orlando's whistle, went out on the stoop.

"*Hola*," he said, coming into the light of the lantern in his kitchen. "What's the matter?"

"There's a bat."

"You want coffee?"

She went and sat on his steps. He came out with two tin cups.

"What's the matter?"

"Nothing, a bat."

"You don't get enough loving maybe?"

"Maybe."

"You tell Orlando about it."

"You're on your rounds."

"I'll just whistle a minute." He blew a blast.

"Why do you whistle? To warn the thieves?"

He laughed. "*Vigilante*s must whistle. Otherwise, their employers might think they are sleeping…Some loving, eh?" He moved closer to her, kissed the side of her neck.

"And your rounds?"

"You wait. I go?"

"No."

"Come with me then."

"All right."

At the top of the pasture, he blew a blast on his whistle, and then spread his poncho under one of the silk cotton trees that marked the division between The *Doña's* property and the *Franceses*. She sat down on it and pulled her own poncho around her. He sat next to her and traced a finger along her jaw.

"Funny girl."

"It's cold."

"I warm you. Tell me something."

"What?"

"You sleep with him too?"

"Who?"

"The other one."

"Willi? No. Funny, us talking English."

"I love the English. I go back there so quick I have a chance. You take me, eh?"

"We aren't going back. It's crazy. You all want to go there."

"Sure, we would go! All of us would go, every miserable son of a *puta*," he said. "Here there is nothing. *Nada!*"

"But you're married," Blanche said.

"That is The *Doña.* That is no matter. The girl belongs here. I send her something. Here, sit closer; take this off here."

He pulled off her poncho and her sweater, and lay beside her, his leg astride her legs. "Beautiful, beautiful. *Don* Carl, I bet he don't appreciate you."

"He did once."

He pulled up her nightgown and pinched her breasts.

"It's *her* he loves, you know."

"Who?" He undid his pants.

"The old woman."

"The *Doña*?"

"Yes."

Orlando was shocked. "But she wouldn't ever…"

"Of course not, it's impossible. That's why he likes it."

He got up. "I'll just whistle…"

"Hurry, it's cold."

"Hurry, she says, the little woman. Yes, I hurry." He blew a blast and crawled back to the blanket. "He is coming, your Orlando, coming."

Carl went alone up the mountain. He found the children at the outdoor table with their homework, and Sonia among the drying coffee beans. The Jeep had not come, but *El Vicepresidente* was still alive. Sergio had got the knack of the nose tube. It was worrisome, yes, that their district and some of their associates were being named in the papers.

"But we go on, *Don* Carl," said Sonia. "We have a crop ready," she indicated the burlap drop cloths covered with ripe coffee beans spread all about her.

Carl told her about Rafa's suspicions.

"Oh, he will never harm us; but it is best to keep from him what we can. We will be discreet. Don't come again unless I send for you."

"But how will we know?" Carl asked.

"There are the newspapers."

"No, we will come, one of us, when we can."

"All right, you are very good to us. The *Doña* will help if there is need. I have given directions to *Don* Willi. The children…"

The morning of *Nochebuena*, the *carnicero* came to the farm up the hill to kill the pig. Carl heard the squeals at five in the morning; he got up. Willi was up already in the kitchen. "Hurry," he said, "I want to see all of this." They climbed the hill behind the stable.

Clouds covered the slopes, rolling through the coffee bushes and eucalyptus trees. They climbed up a slippery path, catching at the clumps of *Argentina* grass. The sun was just behind the *cordillera*; thin rays broke through the pile of purple clouds which would bring the day's storm. At the top of the field, they climbed up to the stone steps below *Los Frances* brick bungalow. On the patio at a long table covered with oil cloth *Doña* Eulalie, her two servants, and their own Olga and Miriam sat chopping messes of cilantro and green onions. Out behind the house, Luciano and the *carnicero* stood in the stable, waiting for the blood of the drawn pig to collect in an aluminum washtub. Just outside, Orlando had built a fire with an improvised spit from which two large kettles were hung. The carcass was skinned and the head cut off and thrown in the boiling water. The steaming intestines were pulled out and washed under the spigot. *Doña* Eulalia brought out the wooden bowls full of chopped herbs and dumped them into the congealing blood in the aluminum tub. This mixture was then ladled into the tied-off gut to make blood sausage. These were boiled in the pot with the head. Next the fatback was removed and sent into the kitchen to be fried for breakfast. Eight o'clock by now, the clouds were lifting. Glittering droplets condensed on the plantains and coffee bushes. Carl and Willi fed the fire with dead wood. *Doña* Luz arrived; Olga brought out hot chocolate, and they sat on milking stools to drink.

The *carnicero* went to work then, stretching the carcass on a platform of rough boards. He hacked off the trotters, which went into the pot, then cut off the two haunches. Eulalia had a huge wooden vat filled with salt water and nitrate ready to receive these. The loins, with the bone removed, were stretched out in long wooden troughs and covered with the same onions and cilantro that had gone into the sausage; then a mixture of beer and orange juice was poured over them.

"These will go in the oven tonight," Eulalia explained to Willi, who was copying down the recipes in a notebook.

The gray clouds piled up like dirty linen, and the wind rose, rattling the leathery plantain leaves. Luciano rigged a tarpaulin over the fire and the woodpile. The sausages were fished out, and Olga carried some of them off to fry in the kitchen. The salivating dogs hung about and were thrown bits of gristle and bone. Thunder rolled; it grew dark, and fat raindrops pattered on the zinc roof of the stable. A child dressed as a pirate ran out of the house:

"Está servido."

They left the fire and went in to sit at the long table at the end of the patio. Olga and Miriam brought plates of *chicharrones*, sausages, and fried plantains. Rain poured off the tiles. "Eat up," said *Don* Jorge. "It will have to last you till midnight."

The great bruised clouds raced overhead; suddenly a white sun broke through. The patter slowed; the drains gurgled. An almond *turrón* was brought and sliced with little cups of black coffee. Miriam, looking wan, cleared the table. Eulalia went to baste the meat. *Don* Rafa took aguardiente to the *carnicero*; and *Don* Jorge offered Will and Carl cigars.

"What a lot of work," *Don* Jorge said, stretching out in a hammock. "My wife gives herself this trouble twice a year. There're plenty of beds, anyone wants a nap."

A series of dark bedrooms opened off the patio. Carl found a small room with an iron bedstead. Two army blankets were folded at the bottom of the bed. He wrapped himself in one of these and fell into the deep sleep that the heavy blankets seemed to induce. In another room, Eulalia's daughter slept beside her suckling child. Rafa slept on an army cot and his wife on Eulalia's big iron bed. The *carnicero* dozed on a bench in the stable.

Carl, waking in the dark room felt stupefied with food and sleep. He went to the spigot and washed his face. Work had begun again. The gelatinous liquid in the kettles was poured through a strainer into five long tin molds; then, what was left behind in the strainer was picked through and the bones thrown to the dogs. The rest: brains, tongue, trotters, chopped fine and stirred into the gelatine. The dying fire was built up again, and one of the hindquarters spitted to roast. The *carnicero* had gone, taking with him a side of fatback, his payment. Luciano tended the meat, basting it with *habanera*, which caused the flames to leap. Rafa had brought out a bottle of *aguardiente*.

"Gives herself this trouble when we could have stuck it all in a freezer down in the city," said *Don* Jorge.

"Used to keep it all salted before the hydroelectric. Didn't taste like much," said Rafa. "Smelled to heaven. Luciano here would remember. You remember how we used to keep meat before the hydroelectric?"

"Yes. My father would smoke it."

"How long would it keep?" Willi asked. "Weeks? Months?"

"More like weeks."

"Troublesome beasts," said Jorge. "I remember I was living in the capital, one of my clerks brought me a pig up the elevator, presented it to me for *Nochebuena.* I had to give half of it to the swindler at the butcher's in order to get it taken care of."

"One thing you can say for up here in the mountains, the *carnicero* takes his side of fatback and a bottle of Cruz Verde and considers himself well paid," said *Don* Rafa. The nephews and two of Eulalia's grandchildren had dressed themselves up as pirates and cowboys and were throwing *estrellitas* into the coffee bushes. The sun dropped behind the *cordillera,* and some rockets from Kilómetro Veinticinco burst among the eucalyptus trees. Orlando and *Don* Alberto made several trips bringing gifts, salads, two roasted chickens.

Don Rafa opened a bottle of Cruz Verde and sliced up a green mango. He and Jorge had begun their serious drinking and didn't touch the bits of Genoa sausage and white cheese, the cups of bread soup that were sent around. The children seemed drunk to Carl, reeling about as harlequins, Cinderellas, pirates. But he realized it must be a phenomenon of his own drunkeness. The little girls tripped on the hems of their long dresses. "Papa, give us *estrellitas.*"

"Papa, when does *el Niño* come?"

"At midnight, *mijo,"* said his father, who was hoeing calmly in *Don* Jorge's garden. Carl took some soup and closed his eyes to steady the world.

"Come," Orlando said to Blanche, pulling her into the trees. "There's no one below."

They slipped and slid down the hillside. He had a bottle of *habanera* with him, which he passed her. "My girl," he said, slipping his hand under her poncho and into her shirt. "No one care if I whistle tonight, eh?" He pinched her breast. She drank the rum, shivering:

"It's cold."

"Warm in my place," he said. "Oven's been on all day."

"Not there."

"Yes, in the bed." They felt their way around behind the stable and through the plantain grove. He lit a match. "Come quick!" He found the lantern and lit it, bringing it into the kitchen and setting it on the floor. He unwrapped her poncho, started on her buttons. Her bowels felt watery. He took off her shirt, undid the waist of her jeans, pulled them down and ran his hands over her belly. "Beautiful, beautiful."

"Sick," she murmured and ran out to the porch and vomited. He came out behind her.

"Oh, Christ, I hate being sick! Go away!"

"*Ahora sí, ahora sí.*" He held her while she hung over retching; then she had to run to the latrine. He followed her with the lantern, stood over her while her bowels turned to water. "Now, now, it passes," leading her back to the bedroom. "Better now, better now, yes."

She lay across the bed. He rubbed her, kissed her all over. "I have you here. I have you in all the beds, in the *Doña's*..."

"Oh, no! God!" She felt better.

"A little drink, just a little." He passed her the bottle. She drank, coughed. He slipped off his clothes, lay beside her, and stroked her pale, inner arms: *"Tan blanca que es, Doña Blanca..."*

"We must go up. I have a bad feeling," Carl said.

"Later. When they begin the firecrackers, and the women are praying." Willi said.

Bursts of red and green rose over Kilómetro Treinta. "Big doings in Kilómetro Treinta tonight," said Jorge, "Luz Marina Rosano was named Queen of the Sugarcane."

"The girl from Zacapa?"

"She was born in Tuxpan. It was on the radio they've turned over the Brigadier's Jeep and there's been a stabbing. A character in a *cantina* said she had silicone breasts."

"What a thing to say about one of our women. Silicone, breasts!"

Olga sent word from the kitchen that the pregnant child had stomach cramps.

"Probably too much *turrón,*" said Berta; she told Olga to have her lie down. "Her time isn't for three weeks yet." She wiped soot from the face of her youngest.

"Is the *Niño* coming?" he asked his mother.

"Not for another couple hours."

"Where is Orlando?" *Doña* Luz asked.

"He's taken himself off somewhere. Probably Kilómetro Treinta."

"*Now* is the *Niño* coming?"

"But *mijo*, it's only two minutes since you asked," said Berta. "Do you know your piece? Say your piece for me."

Mambrú se fue a la guerra
Que dolor, que dolor, que pena.
Mambrú se fue a la guerra.

131

No se si volverá…

The child shouted, and ran away.

At eleven thirty, the younger children were sent to try to bring the men inside without success. They still had the big rockets to throw.

"It is quarter to twelve. We must pray without them," said Luz, leading the children and servants into the veranda.

"But the rockets…" said the nephews, torn.

"The *Niño* cannot come until we pray," said Berta, pushing the children into the room. Carl stood with *Don* Alberto in the dark entryway, hovering, between men's affairs and women's. The *Doña* read the prayers for the last day. One exhausted child lay in her lap. The older children knelt in the front, their faces on a level with Eulalia's rustic stable and its porcelain figures. Behind, stood the servants, their faces lit by the flickering candles. The pregnant child crouched off to one side, clutching her belly.

The *Doña* finished her reading, and Berta's heavy voice began the *Salve Maria's*, rising and falling monotonously.

Miriam groaned and The *Doña* went to her and led her from the room. He wondered where Blanche was. He supposed she might be asleep in one of the bedrooms.

La torre está en guardia
La torre está en guardia.
Quien la destruirá?

The children sang, and Don Alberto looked at his watch. "Midnight," he said.

132

"*El Nino!*" the children shouted. Eulalia, feeling under the skirts of the table, brought out the porcelain figure, which she placed in the straw.

The children, revived from their stupor, tore at the wrappings of the gifts, which were passed out by Berta and Eulalia. "Calmly, calmly!" scolded *Doña* Luz, but she was ignored.

The haunch was brought in, and saffron rice, baked plantains, roast chicken, fried yucca, *tamales* wrapped in banana leaves, fruit salad. The children, revived by their toys, paid little attention to food, and *Don* Rafa and *Don* Jorge still refused to come in.

"No one will know."

Orlando put the lantern down on the floor of the big bedroom. Blanche stood in the doorway, saw herself from the waist up in the big mirror above the dressing table.

"Come." He lay on his back on The *Doña's* bed, waiting. "They are all up there above. How can they know we are here?"

"Why must we?" She said. "Why must we be in this room?"

"Because you're my lady," he said. "My *Doña* Blanca. Come." He held out the bottle.

She drank.

"Lie down here by me."

"No." She held the blanket around her.

"I told you. They are all up there. The men are drunk and the women are praying."

"Turn out the light then."

He turned down the wick. She went to him. Now I am lost, she thought.

133

When the eating was over and people starting to go home, Miriam was discovered bent over the kitchen sink. "*Diós Santo*! Where is Orlando?" Berta cried. He was discovered coming up the hill and sent to take the girl home and fetch Solita.

Carl found Blanche alone on the dark veranda. "What's the matter?"

"Nothing."

"Didn't you want to eat?"

"I…"

"What is it?"

"Something awful is happening."

"To you?"

"To us."

"Where've you been?"

"I went to lie down."

"Are you sick?"

"Yes."

It was three in the morning when they went down the mountain. Orlando was gone off on his bicycle. The girl moaned softly in the back room of the hut. The children were carried off to bed. Luciano and Rafa smoked in the courtyard, finishing off a bottle of Cruz Verde. Carl sat on the stoop. Blanche had gone to bed. Willi came in and put on fresh clothes. "I'm going up."

"Go, yes, go!"

Willi stood in the doorway of the cottage. There were no signs of Christmas here. Sonia sat at the table, and he could see through the doorway that the Similac bottle still hung from the hook that held the mosquito net.

"Nothing," said Sonia. "We do not hear. We had a message two days ago they were to come this morning with a Jeep. We have waited all day."

"Not even a message?"

"Nothing, sit. Sergio sleeps. I am watching."

"Something has happened. Don Willi, Sergio and I will go with the *Americano* if the Jeep comes. But the children are to hide in the cave until we've left. Then they will go to Solita and she will send word to you."

"They are to go to my brother. They are to study and receive scholarships. She must be firm in this, for they do not listen to me…"

Willi frowned. He could think of nothing to say.

"Perhaps, it is not necessary. You can wait some days. If we do not return…"

"I will take them now. Let me take them now."

"No, they would not go. They are serious children, and good. We must respect their wishes in this. They will hide when the Jeep comes and then run to Solita."

"You should come now, with them. Let Sergio go!"

"I cannot, *Don* Willi. You know what I am. What we are."

"Tell me then, if we have no word, and you are gone. Who then?"

"Who?"

"Who then I go to?" Willi reverted to pidgin speech when he talked to Sonia.

"I tell you that and you become too involved, you are in danger like us."

"Tell me more."

"Aye, *Don* Willi!"

"Tell me more."

"The pharmacist at Kilómetro Treinta."

"*Que no aguantooooo!*" groaned the girl.

"So it begins, does it," said Rafa.

"Will it be long?" Willi asked.

"Could be a day or more."

"Noooooooooo! *Que me mata!*"

Willie walked outside of the circle of lamplight. The girl was moving about. Something fell over in the cottage. "I'll take her some rum," said Rafa, going in with the bottle.

It became quiet, and Willi fell asleep for a time in a hammock.

Nearly dawn, the mist rose in tatters. The girl was screaming; Orlando had still not returned. Carl sat on the porch holding his head. *Don* Rafa came out in slippers.

"The old woman will be with another," he said. "Ah, well, it's better without her, I've always felt. I never liked Solita with her injections, putting the infant to sleep, so it forgets to breathe. Olga is up; she will go over."

Something heavy fell over in the hut; the girl shuffled from room to room, bumping into the furniture.

"Mongrel bitch I had once," said Rafa, "…ran in circles, dropping her litter here and there. Red as a fox, dropped one of her whelps in my shoe."

"*Nooooo!*" the girl bellowed, "*Ni un momento mas!*"

"*Aguanta pues, si no hay remedio,*" said Rafa. "In my day, they delivered themselves hanging from a rope tied to the rafters. In hammocks too; that was a trick. No, better without Solita and her ampules. I'm not the only man to say it. It doesn't do to ask the women. You don't ask a woman to be objective."

"*Uy, uy, uy.*"

Something else fell over and broke. Willi went to the spigot and ran some cold water over his face. The patio was filled with a silvery half-light.

"*No, no, no, no!*"

He found a bottle of Ron Viejo and took it over to the other hut. The girl was crouched in a corner of the kitchen, her eyes wild.

"Have this," he said, holding out the bottle, "*Tenga.*"

She wouldn't get up. He found a glass on the floor, filled it and took it to her. She drank it, choked. He gave her more. She drank it, then settled in a heap, moaning. "I'll stay with you, shall I?" Willi said, righting a chair and sitting down. She stared at him. He was speaking English without thinking. Then she began screaming. "No, no, no!"

"You want me to leave?"

She got up and began running again, stumbling over the debris on the floor. He backed out. "I'll get Olga," he said. "You must have someone. Yes, I'll get Olga…"

Olga came out, and the *Doña*, with armfuls of linen. "It won't be yet," Olga said after she had settled the girl in bed. "The child is high in the womb. She is frightened and she is young."

A pale bicycle light wavered below on the road, turned the corner and came slowly up. Orlando walked the bicycle, a figure beside him, wrapped in a blanket.

"She was with someone else," Orlando said. Solita was an ageless Indian with a gray blanket thrown over her shoulders. She carried a worn briefcase. Orlando led her into the hut. "*Basta,*" she said to the moaning girl. "You be quiet." Her dark figure moved about in front of the lamp.

"She'll give her an injection," Rafa said. "She'll settle her."

Willi made coffee. They sat at the table on the porch as the sky lightened. Orlando came out of the hut and sat on the stoop. "It'll be hours," she says.

"*Sí, hombre.* What kept you?"

"She was with a woman in La Florida. There was a haemorrhage."

"Women," said Don Rafa. "I have one *volcán* left. We'll set it off when your son is born."

"Yes, man!"

"Right off the cliff there, over Kilómetro Veinticinco." Don Rafa walked over to the edge of the courtyard and set up the little rocket. "For the little president, eh? That's why Orlando came back to this place where Judas lost his boots. So, his son can be native born, eligible for the presidency, eh?"

"Oh sure!" said Orlando.

"*Uy!*" moaned the girl, "*Uy!*"

"*Te callas, te callas, oye,*" from Solita.

"Have their ways of killing here, too," Blanche murmured behind Carl in the doorway, where she sat.

"Not a place for us, Carl. It's death. I feel it."
"Uy! Uy! Uy!"

"You told her to give her a sedative?" Rafa asked Orlando. "Solita doesn't let them scream for long."

"Fucking talk!"
"Fucking...!"

Rafa turned around to look at Blanche: *"Pero, Doña Blanche..."*

"Fuck you, fuck you all, and fuck you all!" Carl grabbed her, held her from behind.

"Fucking, fucking, fucking, fucking...!"

"She is hysterical. It has been too much. We will go in," said Rafa. "We will go to bed; there is nothing we can do out here."

Solita was sent over to give Blanche an injection. She slept and woke, slept and woke, dreamed of giving birth to a small monkey.

They got up at noon. It was quiet. Willi found Rafa smoking in the garden. "How goes it?"

"Labor stopped. Solita is letting her rest. Later, she will give quinine to start it again."

"All over again?"

"Yes, a dangerous thing."

The ladies came to play hearts and eat *turrón,* but Blanche didn't go over.

She was curled up on the big iron bed, moaning. At times, her moans repeated the timbre and rhythm of the moans that came from next door; for the quinine had been administered and labor had resumed. Carl sat at the foot of the bed trying to read. He wanted to touch Blanche, but she wouldn't let him.

Willi hoed in the beans, to put to some use the restlessness in his muscles that wanted to take him up the mountain. The moans rose and fell, but the exhaustion of the previous night, the repetition of something already lived, took the urgency out of them.

At eight that evening, the child, a boy, was born dead.

"So," said Rafa, coming out from the big house to where they sat on the stoop. "*El Presidentito* is dead. The little president is dead…"

"This one in there," he shrugged a shoulder toward Orlando's hut. "This one might have been a little president…little brown president to promise holidays to the workers, yes…"

Carl went in to Blanche. She was up and dressed. "I'm leaving," she said. She had on her Boston Common polo shirt.

And then it was on the radio that Rafa kept in the stable. The holders of the kidnapped executive had been taken in.

"A Jeep was sent and they were all taken to the capital," Rafa told Willi.

"Yes," Willi said in anguish. "They were expecting it to take them to Purua," he confessed to Rafa. What was the good of concealing things from him any longer?

"Oh God! Oh, God! We thought everything would be all right. How, how?"

"A Jeep was sent; but it was sabotaged. Someone had talked. Two government agents were along."

"And are they killed? Sonia…!"

"Sergio's in prison. The woman and children I don't know. Arms were found…"

"Yes, yes, there were guns. We saw them."

"You were very foolish to go there."

"They were good people."

"I imagine they were."

"Did the man die?"

"He is said to be near death."

"Oh, God! It wasn't them. Himself, he killed himself. They tried to save him."

"A bad diabetic, the papers say."

"Yes. He refused to eat. They sent to the Rurales for a doctor after they had trouble getting him to eat. No one would come. They sent a boy with a nose tube, Sergio put it in himself."

"And you?"

"We couldn't do anything. We were supposed to talk him into wanting to live. His mind was made up. His wife had left him. His son was some kind of misfit. I guess we reminded him of the son. We were worse than useless. And he was already very ill."

"An unhappy event all around. This Sergio will be shot; and others too, whether they helped or not. There will be examples made. It won't do their cause much harm. They're purposely decentralised. That's probably why no one would help."

"The children…We promised Sonia, the children! They were to hide where the arms…"

"They found the arms. They won't be there. You won't find them. This is a more serious matter than you appear to realize. Arms were found. A North American is dead, or almost."

But they went. They had to see. They had to wait three days as the rains were so hard and steady the road washed out. When they got there, they found no one, and the house was burned.

They walked around it, kicking in the ashes. Evidently, it had been torched at the side where the bedrooms were. That part was fallen in; but the fire had burned out, leaving the kitchen intact. There were the two mattresses still on the floor, and the pot of soup and kettle of coffee on the kerosene stove. The children's books and papers were still at the end of the table where the girl had sat; and the two oil lamps the boy had been cleaning.

They climbed the hill at the back. The boards with the branches stapled to them were thrown about, and the crates pulled out and overturned. Books and weapons were gone. Gorky's *La Madre* lay face down in the mud. A dirty child watched them.

"Did they take all of them," Carl asked.

"*Sí, en un Jeep.*"

Blanche was on the steps with the backpacks when they got back. She was going as far as Tuxpan in the car with *Don* Alberto, then on to the capital in *porpuesto*.

A priest had come, was inside the hut with the *Doña*, praying. Orlando was in the plantain grove hammering together a coffin of *palosanto*.

Don Rafa had brought out a bottle of tequila, poured out three glasses: "Never forget they used to bottle it in the same bottle as their cattle purge. Dozens of accidents. Ah, well you've heard that story…"

"She has to go, Willi, you see that?" Carl said to Willi.

"She's sick. She's had too much. 'It's death,' she said; 'There's death here.' She started saying it a month ago, when the hens were dying, now this…"

"Of course, it's their ways, Carl. There's an ancient balance."

Carl could hear the murmured *Salve Marias* from the cottage, and see the shadowy figure of Luz moving about the bed. The child was lying on the kitchen table, he could see, on top of a white tablecloth. The priest's voice was a rumbling counter bass.

"Unfortunate, what's happened, but she'll have another," said Rafa. "Strong girl like her, how she did yell."

After it was all over, they found that Orlando was also gone.

Carl continued to care for the cow. Milking, took him twice as long as it had Orlando, and he also fed and hosed down the sow.

His daytime chores were usually done by noon, when he took a shower and changed into clean clothes that Orlando's woman brought in and put on his bed every day. One of the reasons she was shy and confused around him, he decided, was that he spent all his afternoons at the big house, as if he had been a guest from the city. It was as if his slopping around with the pig was some sort of aberration only a gringo would indulge in.

She did little things like hanging a curtain in his kitchen, and when there were embers from her woodstove on baking day, she would fill the old-fashioned iron with them and press one of his better shirts as if to nudge him up to the level where he belonged.

The *Doña* had finished the Henry Adams and they began reading *Bleak House* in the week before they left for the city.

Then Willi moved up to Sonia's place.

After Carl had done his shopping in Tuxpan, Mondays, he continued on the bus, past the *abasto,* up the mountain to the margin of the farm where Willi was living in an outbuilding. There were only a few items that Willi needed from the town. A carton of Polar Beer, one pack of cigarettes—he smoked one cigarette each evening—salt, matches. For the rest, Willi had Sonia's chickens and the vegetable garden.

"Any news," Carl would ask, and there would be a hint by way of the pharmacist that the children had found their way to a caretaking family, of a plan being conceived. Finally, there was confirmed information of another kidnapping in a distant province, intended as a swap for the mother's freedom. Sergio had been shot against a wall in Charagua.

Willi was holding the property together for Sonia. He was weeding her garden and keeping her hens and harvesting some coffee which Carl would eventually sell in Tuxpan and the money would be put into an account for Sonia to have when she was free.

And he had found clay in the cut the backhoe had carved out of the mountainside to link up a new farmhouse to the main road. He showed it to Carl, wonderful shades of terra cotta and cream and lilac shovelled into plastic tubs; and a pile of sun-baked bricks, he was making in a wooden mold. First, he would build a wood fired oven with these bricks, then he would fire bricks to build a proper kiln. He would build himself a studio then and make sculptures from the same clay, the idea of them already in his head.

"Like the first man," Carl had said.

"Yeah, soon I won't need the cigarettes. I'm weaning myself."

"If Sonia comes back, I'll marry her," said Willi. We'll get her kids back. "We owe her those kids."

"Yes, we do," said Carl gravely.

"Meanwhile I'm working," Willi said. He stood up and led Carl into the hut he used as sleeping quarters and studio. There, still unfired, was a large reclining figure of Blanche.

"In all her glory," said Willi.

Soror Mystica

Henrietta Rose puts on her boots. It's Christmas Eve, the day before her first party in thirty years.

If you can believe this, Henrietta Rose was once a famous party giver in foreign Capitals. Now, in her come-down state from the days she consumed bottles of Grand Marnier that took 30 years to age in half an hour, she is a woman living alone in a HUD subsidised apartment on Loomis Street in Waltham, Massachusetts.

Christmas Eve, everything that a person living alone needs: buses, banks, the post office, the public library, is closed. Well, buses are running on half schedule. Of course, stores are open, full of frenzied shoppers. She shuns these. They give her panic attacks.

She fastens up her boots carefully. It won't do to fall today, before her party, then makes her way to bus stop with her two canes. As she reaches the corner, the Chinese boy, who lives next door, waves and wavers on his bicycle down the center of the lane. "You ought to wear a helmet," Henrietta calls.

"Oh, yes," he grins, and stops to greet her. He was in some student demonstration, the Fahey woman told her, and had to escape the country with some help from Brandeis University. Now he's cleaning houses till he starts his studies.

"Seriously," she says slowly and distinctly. "I was hit once when I used to ride."

It was in Troy. She ran into another woman on a bicycle and flew into a bush.

"Oh, yes." He grins politely, hasn't an idea what she's saying.

"And you ought to have a light. I see you go at night."

"Yes, yes." He makes a little bow.

She gives up. Listen. She fumbles in her purse and finds the notebook and the pen she keeps, and writes, Come tomorrow for dinner at three p.m.

He reads and understands: "Yes, oh yes. Thank you. Thank you."

She sees her bus coming and waves frantically; he's about to pass her.

"What's your name?"

"Chang."

Chang, she writes it down in her notebook as soon as she's settled in her seat. She will buy Chang a helmet for Christmas. Another guest, but with the leaf and extra chairs she actually can seat two people more. She plans to shop at Wallex Plaza on her way home. Seated on the bus, she thinks happily about her painting.

Her painting waiting for her, behind some moldy prayer books in the basement of the Episcopal Church...

The house in West Boylston with the walls torn away so you can see inside.

And, like the early Christians who meet in the basements of churches, where she gained her precious six years of sobriety, Warren's Red Feather painting class for the elderly infirm that meets in the basement of the Episcopal Church never cancels for any holiday.

She is peopling the exposed rooms in the house in West Boylston: Lutie in the living room smoking, legs crossed gracefully, hair piled up. In the kitchen, she'd begun a figure of a woman working at a sink, and wasn't sure last Thursday if it's Hulda Engbretsen or Nummie. But she realizes now, of course, it is Miz Lili, as they were supposed to call her, or Nummie as they actually called her.

Lately, she likes to think of Nummie. Nummie loved the kitchen. For all her gentle upbringing, she spent more time in the kitchen than in drawing rooms. Where Lutie had been a fretful housekeeper, Nummie used to relish stationing herself in the kitchen, directing the cooks and maids, jumping, herself, to chop things finer than they could, to taste and season, whomp the bread dough with an energy exceeding any cook she ever had.

Nummie did it out of joy. She could have changed her station anytime with Hulda Engbretsen, with her own cook at home in Louisville, and still been happy.

The same with handwork, yes, she can remember Nummie setting out a quilt, the little houses, cut out freehand, trees with birds in them, and children jumping rope cut from scraps of printed cloth and sewed with tiny, patient stitches, joyous work.

Like mine, she takes a deep, slow breath. I might have learned it anytime from her...But then I might have died a drunk like Lutie, never learning...

"Well," says Warren when she walks in late because of the buses. We thought that you're like all the other ladies, doing what-they-call-it, last minute shopping.

"Well, I plan to, but mine is very rapid." She fumbles with the tubes in such a hurry, now she knows who the kitchen figure is, her darling Nummie. She has to calm herself and take deep breaths.

It's only Mike and Warren today; the tole painter—troll painter—as Mike calls her, and the other water color ladies absent. Mike and Warren are discussing World War II as usual. Not a sign of holiday decoration, it reminds her of the time she couldn't bear a holiday. Only now can she bear a holiday. Hence her party.

The figure in the armchair, Lutie, is just right, the airy posture, and the absent stare of the large eyes. She makes the figure so you can see right through it, for Lutie was often absent. They would see her upturned pumps the bottom of a stair, and then she would be sent away for one of her 'rests'.

Henrietta makes the kitchen figure, more substantial, bigger than the refrigerator, she's standing next to…that's all right. Perspective is something Mike worries about, but Warren encourages her to ignore. Warren was born in The Bleachery, that warren of Jewish Bolsheviks, went to war and came back and learned to paint at the New School. Henrietta Rose knows what she's doing he scolds Mike. There was art before there was perspective.

And Nummie had a big frame. You saw it when she lost the weight at start of that long illness, when her breasts, released from corsets, sagged past her middle.

"You really want her that big?" Mike says behind her.

Oh, yes, she was big, important…

149

Who's that guy up in the attic? Warren wants to know. And the things flying out of the window...

"Oh, my brother Mounty. We engaged in alchemy up there...And contests." She'll get to him next.

After the alchemical messes and the investigation of falling bodies, Mounty turned to contests in the newspapers and magazines. It brought them back together briefly, for she had to participate of course; it increased the odds. Henrietta was valuable as she was clever at answering riddles and finding hidden bunnies in forest scenes.

They never won; it flummoxed Mounty. Must be the mail, he spent his money on special delivery sometimes, and nothing. Statistically, we have to win sometime. The odds...

And that was where he ended up, a statistician. He worked for firms that played the market, bonds she thinks it was.

She lost him somewhere, up there in the attic, during the puzzles sometime. What did they need money, prizes, for? They had as many toys as any child could want.

She cannot think where Mounty might have saved himself...where she...How careless she had been, and stupid.

Mounty won a scholarship to the London School of Economics, and married there, another student: Lovely girl from Cornwall. A redhead; and they'd had a pretty daughter with a head full of copper ringlets. Had they left him, or he, them?

Her own young family: how beautiful they'd been; there, she might have stuck. Had they been undone by Lutie's evanescences? They might equally have been held fast by Nummie's strong presence in the kitchen...

Mounty, she was going to Mounty after Carol.

She'd been to Plum Island with Carol's ashes, tossing them into the withdrawing froth, and in the morning Jeannie put her on the Boston & Maine to Fitchburg. To Mounty in the big house in West Boylston. The last part never happened. She recalled the train was cold, or perhaps it was only her weakness after those ten months with Carol on the road…seeking some substance—the Leaf of the Yew—to halt her cancer in Seattle. Then in Mexico—The Pit of the Apricot, was it? In any case, she'd tried to stand up, pull her coat down from the rack, and her legs had failed her. An evanescence like one of Lutie's famous, The Korsakoffs.

At first, she couldn't walk. The present erased as soon as it happened. And she was four years sober. It was like one of those WW two torpedoes netted by Gloucester fishermen years later.

Childhood memories were pleasantly intact: The big house in West Boylston, herself as a young mother, herself atop an elephant in India. Not all of it. For then, there were the blackouts. When did they menstruate, when did they sprout pubic hair?

She must see him. She'd consulted enough doctors over the years with these questions. Instead of bothering Mounty about his drinking, she might have inquired with him where this closing in process, this letting go of spouses and children, had begun with each of them.

Flying out of the attic, she paints a row of envelopes addressed to contests. She wonders how they could have been so intent, so organized, as children; and so careless as adults…

The last time she visited Mounty she remembers the parlours, the great kitchen of the house, in West Boylston, blocked with old dresses, offset presses, cranberry bins, ancient linotype machines, cookie tins and breadboxes, toppling piles of books, and sloping avalanches of old *National Geographics* on the floor in corners of the rooms. He was running a newsletter for people wanting to exchange collections of Iron Side tapes for books by Tasha Tudor; vintage gas ranges; for horror comics, antique cradles, Shirley Temple dolls, antique soda bottles, English licence plates...and all of it passed through the house, which he hardly ever left. His air of brisk business would have fooled her if she hadn't stayed around to see him subsiding like the piles of magazines into a stupor in late afternoon. She was in one of her early, lost, attempts at sobriety, and talking more about it than she should, and tried to tell Mounty that he could get it back: the wife, the daughter, job on the exchange...if only he could stop the drinking; but that Mounty of the job on the exchange she had really experienced very little, being in foreign parts so long. That Mounty couldn't be recalled; instead, she seems to recall encountering the old Mounty of her childhood, that she actually heard him try to interest her on a text on *alchemy.*

No, she probably dreamed this; but his talk of his swapping activities—the swapping newsletter—had something redolent of perpetual motion machines, of the conversion of base matter into precious...

There is a rummage sale upstairs in the church hall. She finds a used helmet and also a bike light, and a perfectly new set of colored pencils for Sheila's child, all for three dollars. Goes home in high spirits with the money she's saved. Mounty will come. Mounty must come. She gets home and spoons the marinade over her leg of pork, then calls him to renew her invitation. He hasn't committed. He doesn't get out much...

"You must," Henrietta begs.

He'll see.

"Mounty, come..." she says, attempting to bridge all the years, all the failures. She hears him clear his throat.

"I'll try," he says.

"Come early," she says, knowing how his afternoons are, subsiding, like the piles of books and bottles surrounding him into a stupor... "The earliest train. I'll have someone pick you up."

In bed, she finishes a story by Herman Melville in an old college text book she found in the Natick storage where Tom had taken her to get some chairs for her guests. It's all defaced by her callow freshman observations in purple ink and an immature hand she forgets she ever had: Purity, Influence of Emerson? Evil, Innocence, and blah, blah.

She had loved these books. Lutie never knew the gift she'd given her, sending her to college, even if it was just to get a suitable father for her children.

And here's her old copy of Mrs. Dalloway.

Clarissa Dalloway, oh yes!

Clarissa Dalloway is on the brink of her party, as Henrietta Rose is on the eve of hers.

Charles calls her at ten. She's already in bed with Clarissa Dalloway. He will come. If he doesn't show up, it's because his car has broken down. Charles is her eldest. He has the family disease. She's trying to support him living in an unheated cabin in the upper reaches of New York State. He's the only one of four, since Carol died, who still talks to her.

If they all come, she will have enough chairs but not enough room at the table. She will have to serve buffet. Buffet changes the character of a party, she well knows. It might be an advantage for this particular event; she will be able to circulate and enliven any dull sub-groups. It is a strategic advantage to a hostess not to be held in a fixed position at a table, where one is helpless to rescue any guests sunk in dullness at the far end of the table.

Clarissa Dalloway on the brink of her party. How true it is, the forebodings, as her party begins. Always Henrietta had these sinking moments.

And then, someone in Clarissa's rooms distractedly bats a curtain blowing in at a window; and this is a signal her party is a success. Of course, the glowing silver, the silk upholstery, has become a mere background...The curtain is something one can push around to get comfortable. Oh, it's thrilling to read. How could she know? Such truth!

Clarissa wants of Peter Walsh something similar to what Henrietta wants from Mounty. Does she find it as the party progresses? No, it seems not. She has no time. "Later, later," she must tell old friends. And the two unconventional ones, Peter and Sally, meet up and seem to agree that Clarissa is a dry social stick, while they are still alive and open to adventure...

But, but...We know how Clarissa once felt about Sally Seton. We know Clarissa's joy as she breaks into her fifty-second year: gathering them all together, standing them upright in the vase like so many roses she will paint.

Henrietta Rose hardly sleeps; Tom will come at ten, she thinks; he will pick up Mounty. Charles could come any time. *What will these people find to say to each other? How will she explain Tom, who is one year, three months and four days sober at last count and who drives her in his battered truck to meetings, to Charles?*

Of course, it won't be till the last moment she can plan on Charles's—or Mounty's, or anybody's—appearance or non-appearance, so plans must be kept fluid and the table not set till the end. The pork done early and served cold...Yes. Yes. She gets out of bed and writes it in her notebook:

Buffet style.

And her wisdom is confirmed when, sometime after two, the phone rings, and she hears the wan voice from the bottom of a well.

"It's Debbie."

Oh, dear God! When phones ring in the early hours like this, her head is always filled with thoughts of gore and mayhem.

"I'm downtown." I got the last train...She has forgotten who this person is. Henrietta forgets, the Korsakoff's...Everything, she must write in a notebook. My name is Henrietta Rose, I am seven years and eight months sober, and I live in a HUD subsidised apartment on Hadley Street. And blah blah blah.

"Can I come?" The girl says, "I'll walk."

The goats, she thinks. Something about goats.

"I'll just sleep on the couch...I didn't drink."

This last reassures Henrietta. "I'll leave the door open."

She gets up and pulls blanket and pillow out of the closet, unlocks the door, and falls asleep.

In the morning, she's forgotten the conversation, is shocked to find the body on her couch; cries out and wakes the girl.

"I called; you said to come. I didn't drink…" says Debbie, sitting up.

"Twill be your theme in glory," sings Henrietta, thinking of the old hymn.

"You said to come."

"Oh, I'm sure I did. I didn't write it down. We'll have some coffee. Today is my big day, I'm throwing a party…" she grins.

Meat in oven says her agenda. She spoons the marinade over for last time, then puts on the coffee.

The girl is fumbling in her backpack. "That smells good…" I knew I should call…somebody in the…

Meetings.

Meetings, yes. He even gave me numbers, Tom, the person you intro…

"But you did, you called me, and you didn't drink."

They laugh.

"I was so crazy." A social worker came to see how I was doing with these children, THAT AREN'T MINE. That belongs to my boyfriend who went off and left all of us. And one of them kept crying and falling down, and got an egg on its head and I couldn't pick it up—the woman's standing in the way—and she picks it up acts like she's some kind of savior to these children I'm trying to take care of, who…

"Who aren't yours."

"And yes, I started screaming that at her, and so she says they'll have to take them; there are too many dogs and goats; it isn't sanitary. When they took us down to file a complaint against us, I was rolling on the floor and kicking at some Formica counter till my foot went through it, then, while they were phoning for police, I just ran out the back…"

"I did try to take care of those kids," she says more calmly.

Henrietta can't remember who these kids are, and how the girl came by them; but the goats sound familiar. She sets some coffee and toast on the table, sits down opposite her and looks into her face. A teary and disordered face, but sober, she can see.

"None of it matters," she says. "I used to take a drink sometimes, so that, I told myself, I could remain a lady. That was the sheerest folly... You have to explore the depths of the unladylike—as you are doing right now—" says Henrietta Rose in her present wisdom.

She hopes that Tom will put in an appearance soon. "I'm having a party today," she tells the girl. "It must be meant that you should come."

"Oh, but I shouldn't stay."

"I have some people I'm trying to get back. Some of them are related to me, like my grandson, Owen. I've been practicing on him, and some others are some people I find interesting and hopeful: Tom, who needs a woman like me, who won't marry him, and you must promise not to marry him either..."

"Oh no! I wouldn't!"

But Henrietta doesn't trust her. "Does Debbie know how to peel potatoes?"

"Not really."

"Oh well, we'll have instant instead." She has to start her gelatine with fruit.

Then Mounty calls.

Since Tom hasn't arrived yet, she must send Debbie back down on the Lexington bus to collect him. What is he wearing?

"An old blue chesterfield, rimless glasses, not much hair, she tells Debbie. Try to grab him and get right back on the bus. Just call out you're looking for a Mr. Mounty Pierce. She sends her off with a borrowed hat and scarf."

He's come! And before Debbie can return with Mounty, Charles comes and stands around the kitchen drinking coffee with Tom, talking about the fuel line on his truck. She gets the green beans in the refrigerator and tries to collect herself. Mounty's come. She looks out the window and it's snowing, reminding her of West Boylston in winter.

The house in West Boylston was a place she got lost in until she was four.

The corridor passed from the enormous, old-fashioned kitchen with the table painted blue in the center—so large you couldn't imagine it coming through any door. Then a series of little rooms to the narrow service stair, which went steeply up two turns; and past the little bedroom where Nummy slept. Once when she was very young, it disappeared, the corridor, the stairway. And no one to tell it to or help her...Mounty in the hospital, having out his adenoids.

When he came home, the corridor reappeared. They resumed predations on the kitchen, carrying up uneaten bowls of oatmeal, cups of chocolate, bowls of raw oats or rice, pungent liniments, eucalyptus smelling salves. Past Hulda's room, another stair, no turning to it, steeper, then along another corridor, with wallpaper, of hunting scenes...a closet. Here they kept one great crock, into which Mounty sometimes let her measure in the latest ingredient, hopefully the one to roil and transmute the mixture.

Into what? In later days when they could read, it was to gold. Base elements to gold, for they were alchemists. Or Mounty was. The roiling to her somehow connected to the danger undergone, the theft, itself, the catalyst. And the hoped-for product, for her, was not gold, but rather some organic mystery.

You must pee in it; he told her as they stood over the mess.

No, no, I can't! It's disgusting! she cried, but she knew she could. She knew that the request was thrilling. He must leave the room then. He did, and she squatted and provided the urina puerorum.

But the boy was disgusted from that day forward, and the Artifex and the Soror Mystica no longer linked left hands and grasped the rose.

It's no use, he said. When there's no way, we can have a fire to boil it. So, after that, it was she alone who tended the seething, organic mess, while he turned his restless boy's attention to the inorganic, the obdurate. He collected rocks. He became fastidious about his person. Seething and roiling were stilled, and Mounty's restless mind had turned to physics: Falling bodies, hers and his, were tested from the many roofs accessible to their bedroom windows, the opposition to gravity of their mother's flowered parasol, their father's several sober black umbrellas, unfurled...

They grasped the Rose.

That's how she'll paint the pair in the attic!

Then Mounty comes; he's shy with Debbie, with the others; and he looks very old. She tries not to be shocked. His

159

eyes seek hers; why must there be such confusion if it's I you want to see? is his appeal.

But later, later, she signals. See my life; this is my new life, these people...

And the meat must come out; and coats taken to the bedroom, and the cranberry punch set out, and the celery and olives. And now Chang has come; his eyes also seek hers, but such is the nature of these mixes of hers, their unknown factors, that it turns out that Mounty in his solitude has taught himself Mandarin. Oh, he always could amaze her. And so, he and Chang are soon deep in conversation on the little love seat she's brought from Natick and put in the alcove by the double window, Chang's pocket dictionary open between them.

Jason, then, comes in with Owen...Why did Sheila come separately? She left early pick up her daughter at her ex-husband's family. But both of them look dangerous and Debbie—who as recently as yesterday was kicking in partitions of a social service agency—applies herself to soothe. And Tom, is orbiting around Debbie, fixed as any asteroid, in spite of all he's ever learned. Whatever happens, they probably won't drink is all that Henrietta can predict. How could she have feared that Debbie wouldn't bring Mounty? You always thought the best of other drunks, you held them up...Even the most hopeless can surprise.

But Jason must, and Mounty must; a discrete bottle of Hennessy's and some glasses stand behind her bowl of cranberry punch. Henrietta calmly casts her eye over it and all the rest:

The potatoes, generously reconstituted with evaporated milk heated up again with butter, and the vegetable medley tossed into a white sauce, and the fragrant pig cooled down to a perfect temperature for slicing. She calls Tom to carve it. A pan of its juices bubbles on the stove; she pours it into Lutie's old gravy boat and carries it in to the table.

It's served, she calls, and pushes Chang and Mounty toward her table. It all looks fine to her. Nothing tastes, as usual; but she takes a plate to one of little tables Sheila's loaned her and feeds herself absently, wishing she could listen in on Mounty, but knowing she'd inhibit them in their bilingual groping. Owen, across the room, looks pale but handsome in a figured sweater, probably an early gift. He's stretching upward, as his mother Carol did when she was twelve or so, the long bones, the fine lifted jaw. The Rose looks. Carol had the Rose looks. It was so hard to see her losing them one by one there in those last days in Mexico. Come to me, she calls him, tall, pale flame like figure, away from the heavy child with her dark curls who is sinking into the sofa, away from his teasing. The child will probably never become his stepsister. How dreadful it is, the children waiting around their entire precious childhoods while the adults in charge of them sort themselves out. Sheila is a nice person, but if she won't stick, and take Carol's place…Henrietta likes her but can't waste time on her.

Owen comes, and folds himself at her feet. "You're growing so tall. And that sweater is very flattering," she tells him.

"I hate it," he says. "It isn't my taste."

"What is your taste?"

"Black," he says. "All my clothes black. And my hair long."

"Like my friend Tom."

161

Owen studies Tom, who is standing in the kitchen doorway. "I like his boots."

"I used to find him rather shocking," she muses. "Now I hardly notice his taste."

"How come he's your friend?"

"He takes me to meetings in his truck. He's been taking me to get my furniture out of storage."

"And that's his chick?"

"You mean Debbie? Well, that just happened, I'm afraid. I invited them both. It might have been a mistake…"

"And how do you know her?"

"She calls me up when she's in trouble. She was in quite a jam yesterday, so she came here and slept."

"And why does she call you?" He's clearly intrigued.

"I wonder that myself. I must think about it. I mean we're both drunks, but there are lots of other drunks she could have called besides me…Whole basements full of them."

"Basements?"

"Where we meet, like the early Christians."

"You mean you drink together?"

"No, no. We try together not to drink." She's tempted to expand here, but decides not.

"I hate Newton," he says. "I wish I could live here."

"Newton schools are very good. You'll be grateful when you go to college."

If he ever does. He's in special classes because of his maladjustment, taking meds for an episode of psychosis. Finding his own meds too. In the streets, she suspects.

"I went a whole semester without ever finding my homeroom. When they found out, they put me in a prison with the mental cases, and we do art all day. Anything I learn, I learn by myself in the library. Sheila thinks they should put me with the smart kids."

"Sheila seems pretty sensible…I spend a lot of time with mental cases myself. It doesn't do any harm. But you should be getting an education. Art was something you had to get around to after the other stuff, like reading *Mrs. Dalloway,* she believed. Dad says I'm mental. Mom's whole family is mental."

He's probably just manipulating her, she thinks.

"I don't want to talk about it," he says.

No, not a holiday subject. And yet she's glad he's circling around her, testing her; he'll maybe call her up out of his depths some night. Like Debbie.

Of course, it was in the family. Lutie was a scandal on a grand scale, in spite of being such a lady, and there were tales of two great uncles ended up in madhouses. They kept Lutie going by periodically sending her for 'rests', and she'd return to family seeming like someone who's been rescued from some harrowing brush with they didn't know what, but who now was 'fine', a convalescent; she'd spend most of day sitting up in bed with pretty bed jackets on, and the children could each spend a half an hour with her being read to or allowed to look at her jewelry boxes, or her photograph albums; and she would once again sit at the table opposite their father, and make her witty observations about people they knew, and laugh in her ladylike way behind her napkin, and serve up the plates as they were brought in by Hulda Engbretsen, and the dessert, which was always something special because Lutie was back.

Lutie, in her soft dresses at the piano…She launched tantalisingly into various sonatas and rhapsodies she'd learned up to the hard parts, stopping in the middle of a phrase of Brahms or Beethoven. When Henrietta's time for lessons came, she made a point of learning the hard parts first.

No, Lutie wasn't likely to lift the lid of that hermetic pot where she and Mounty roiled and fermented, sublimated into the adults they played at being.

She moves on to put out the cake Sheila brought, longing suddenly to talk to someone her own age, to Mounty, before he breaks into the Hennessey bottle, still unopened. He and Jason probably providing their own little bottles, of the variety that fit in jacket pockets.

She finds Mounty talking now to Charles, while Chang is looking at a book he's pulled from her bookcase. Jason is sitting all by himself in the alcove. Time for a little hostess intervention.

She takes her little gifts from under tree; she's slipped checks into cards for Tom and Debbie, so has something for everyone, but Mounty. She really didn't believe he'd come.

"We'll spend billions to excavate it centuries later, I thought one day, when I was driving around to garage sales," Mounty is saying to Charles.

"Yeah," Charles breaks in. "Listen, once when I was cleaning out this house, this woman...*A book*, I thought, *a coffee table book about garage sales*...With mostly photographs. Someone ought to do it. I've thought of doing it myself!"

Their precious junk, she thinks. *Can such a thing as a love of junk be enclosed in a gene?*

She starts to distribute the gifts. Sheila has brought some of the children's gifts, and a beautifully wrapped box for Henrietta, so there are a great many. And little by little, they all fall into the ritual, sitting facing the sapling with the birds in it, and opening their surprises. She is most excited about her gift to Chang, watching him awkwardly take off the paper and examine the lamp, which is the kind that fits against the wheel and generates its own power.

He must put it on immediately, she tells him; and asks Tom if he will help. The bike is in the hallway just downstairs, so all the men troop down. She and Sheila clear some of the plates, and she hears her party settle into its rhythm of calm and excited voices, of younger ones banging in and out and looking for tools in drawers. She takes a cup of coffee then. Coffee always tastes. And a slice of the plum cobbler Sheila's brought. She can taste it too, delicious. She has a second piece and says to Sheila, who's standing at the sink and running hot water over plates, that she wishes she could stay with Jason. For Owen's sake.

"Of course, if you're so terribly unhappy…He's not your child. It just seems you're more…flexible than his father. And Owen does seem to care for you."

"Jason does care about him," Sheila says.

"Of course, and I know his mother was just as awkward as Jason in trying to do something for him, and then her illness…"

"Oh, Henrietta!"

"Well, it was just the wrong time in his life, for them to give up on each other…And now you two giving up…"

"But he's not the only child this ever happened to, and I think he's playing on everyone's sympathy, and we shouldn't let him do that."

"Yes, you're right. And the worst thing is that his mother went off a world away to die, and it must be this huge blank

165

to him. I hope I can tell him about it sometime. Carol wanted me to. I think it's why she forgave me everything and went off with me to Mexico. At first, we were looking for a miracle, but at the end, she wanted me to carry something back to her child."

Sheila puts a plate very gently into the sink. "No matter what happens, I'll stay in touch." I promise.

But here is Chang to thank her for his gift. She lays a finger on his temple. "Now you wear the helmet," she tells him; and he nods effusively. "I know a girl who had an accident, and a helmet saved her brains…"

He nods and smiles; Mounty has been standing by listening to this. "How old do you think Chang is?" He asks her.

"Oh, maybe twenty-one…"

"He's thirty-four. He used to teach philosophy at a university, until they sent him to harvest potatoes."

"Oh, many potatoes," Chang puts in, "and we must eat them too, without any salt or oil even, only potatoes, for three years."

"Oh, dear!"

"I cannot eat potato again, not ever," he says.

"And I made potatoes…" she begins, and feels inadequacy of her response. What can one say? And was that all you had to eat?

"Oh yes, potatoes. All."

But he is smiling and his face is rosy, calm.

Ah, yes. What else was one to say with such a small vocabulary? Probably, Mounty could pull a nuanced answer out of Chang. She'll have to limit herself to saving his skin from traffic along the Lexington Road.

"When did you find the energy, the leisure, to learn Mandarin?" she asks Mounty. "Brains, I mean of course," Henrietta amends. "Ah, Mounty, I don't know you...I don't know you...So many years..."

"Yes."

"I think all the time about when we were children. What were we doing, stirring up all those messes, jumping out of trees...?"

"We were recapitulating the history of our race, of humankind," I'd say.

"Whatever do you mean?"

"Well, the early belief in magic, then alchemy; and, finally, the dawn of reason, science..."

She is thoughtful, watching him. He hasn't started drinking, and his hands, she notes, are tensely clasped behind his head.

"And you think all children do the things we...?"

"We were allowed a certain latitude, we were gifted perhaps, in some small measure." He unclasps his hands to wave his right one above his head. It trembles slightly, and he wedges it back behind his head.

"But I...I don't believe I ever believed in magic," she says. "I just thought if you mixed enough things together, something would happen...Remember when you started sending off to contests, Well, I had a similar notion about the potions we mixed up: you put enough...substances together, something would ferment. Now, was that irrational magic? Something did happen. All kinds of smells and colorful moulds and bubbling did occur..."

"But it never turned to gold," he says.

"I never thought it would!" she cries. "Did you? So, it was magic to you, then science, a classic recapitulation," she says; "but not for me; I stopped off somewhere short of science, but it wasn't magic either...Curious. Maybe women don't, you know, recapitulate..."

Zeppelins...Mounty muses. "The technology of lighter than air ships was the most promising thing around when I was in the first and second grade; by the time I was in boarding school, they'd given up the whole caboodle. World War II. And no one ever equalled the Germans. It might have been a different story if they'd won. These cargo planes they have today, most inefficient transport ever was invented...Like giant ocean liners, the zeppelins they had projected. Room for every luxury..."

"I travelled once, in one of these jets they have, he went on; I didn't know where they thought you were supposed to put your arms and legs for six or seven hours...Never travelled again."

As far back as grammar school they'd parted ways, she thinks. *Can I have magnified those early years out of all proportion? Mounty had been more animated talking with Charles about antique music boxes, than just now, for all her urgency.*

As usual, he'd sought to settle her puzzlement by one of his pronouncements: A classic recapitulation; that had been their childhood for him.

A classic dipsomaniac, she'd been called by that man in the Newton meeting. Well, that had the merit of being true. She's not sure about Mounty's pronouncement; and now he's dozing off.

Oh, but I am a hard woman! He came. He has not taken a drink, or very little, or his hands would not be shaking. *How can I come at him with these matters over which I obsess because they are the only intact memories I have, and expect him, who hasn't necessarily thought about his childhood in years, to have ready answers for me?*

"Forgive me, Mounty," she breathes.

"Umph," he says.

Later, later, Clarissa Dalloway told herself in the midst of her party. We have tomorrow to talk. We have years to talk, Henrietta Rose tells herself, and turns her attention back to her party.

The Painter's House

She must have somewhere of her own, she thought when she arrived back in New Jersey, a little space of her own: So, after she had lighted for the moment in the spare room of her parents' new house, she turned off the highway toward the river to shady streets of Island Heights, a place where her family used to vacation, and asked at The Deli in the little center of the town if they could tell her of a place that rented rooms.

Just down the road. The Studio, it's called. There's a sign, they told her. She passed the tall Victorian houses with the jig sawed gingerbread eaves like maiden aunts with lacy undergarments showing, craning up to glimpse a bit of estuary. There remained a few of the fragile little wooden summer houses that her family used to rent, but it was a year-round community now. Just above the marina it was, a large red house with great trees around. She mounted a spacious porch filled with ferns and rockers and knocked on the door. A yellow haired woman with a weathered face opened a dark green door. The same green as the rockers. "Welcome to the studio of John Frederick Peto," she said.

She followed the woman down a dark corridor, and up a winding stair to a small white bedroom with a big bed covered in a white spread, and woodwork of the same green as the porch. Over the bed was a painting of a battered brass cup hanging on a scratched and abraded door of the same dark green. Peto green, it was called she learned later. She took this room and moved in, throwing a Mexican rug she'd brought with her over the armchair, and placing a red heating pot on the table for her coffee, and the computer in the closet, leaving the door open with a small chair in it for her office. Her clothes, she arranged in the tall bureau. Home, again, in New Jersey, where she hadn't lived in forty years.

She was used, by then, to living in rooms, with few possessions: just her books, some pictures and the computer that had replaced the word processor that had replaced the yellow electric typewriter that had replaced the Smith Corona that she bought as soon as she graduated and began to be a writer. All this she had come down to after the divorce and the sale of the eight-room house in the exurbs of Boston. Then the jobs, to keep them going until the children moved out, and this last job, she had just lost, which came with a room, from which she's been fired. The sting was fresh those days.

There had been nowhere else to go. Jobs were scarce and there was nowhere to live while she looked. Besides, her father was ill, probably dying. It made sense to go home,

Home was not where it used to be, Crossbrook Road: Crossbrook Road which ended in a dirt path and some basement holes dug for houses that were never built and were full of snakes, then the little brook surrounded with skunk cabbage and jack in the pulpit. After you crossed it, there continued as a dirt road which resurrected itself in pavement and another neighborhood like hers and a few houses. She never explored there, but assumed it was a street like her own, where boys were wicked, and mothers screamed their children's' names out at dusk to come home out of the woods where they played, Crossbrook Road. There in the big old kitchen, her mother and aunt made fun of the old Swedes of their family, and talked about people they knew with dreadful diseases like cancer, and made her stand on the table to have her dresses hemmed and gave her home permanents at the sink. Then home had moved first to a bigger more modern house in Bernardsville, where her brother grew up, then down to the shore where they used to go and swim in Barnegat Bay and catch crabs they threw in boiling pots that jumped out already pink and scrabbled across the sandy linoleum floor of the tipsy little house they rented. Well, not exactly there, but close by, in a leisure community for active seniors. Her father had been an active senior till his cancer returned.

Not quite ready to face that, she examined her new place of her own.

Down the hall from the room, was a small old-fashioned kitchen where she could keep some food and heat it on a stove. Downstairs was a big modern kitchen where the summer guests were given splendid breakfasts by the petite woman, Joy, who was John Frederick Peto's granddaughter. Just off the kitchen, and down four steps was 'The Studio' of the painter, kept more or less as he left it by his wife, daughter Helen, and now his granddaughter. *I have seen this before*, she thought, *looking at the large sunken room, with the corner where he painted seated on a Chippendale chair, the rafters hung with musical instruments, the dining table, and all around the objects he painted. Chipped pitchers, old mugs, copper basins, and stringless violins.*

When? How? The Gaulkins, maybe, from Crossbrook Road. The boy who made her read Trotsky's speeches. They were the ones who told her family of this little vacation town on the Toms River, invited them once to visit them in the place they stayed. It could have been this place…There was no way to confirm this.

Downstairs were some good prints of more paintings, and a few originals. A painting of the window of a humble little store window with its display of barley sticks, and a wooden toy horse and a sign offering a room for an absurdly low rent, a crooked candlestick and some old books about to fall off a table, torn fragments of letters you could read if you tilted your head, a number plate shifted off its moorings to reveal a bit of cheesy paint underneath, a burned match, a rusted nail. Still lives, but they weren't still, things were about to tumble over, find their own equilibrium. And they were somehow inhabitants of this house—not the modern kitchen at the back, but some old disappeared kitchen.

Mostly every day she spent helping her mother. There were chores made unnecessarily difficult, like taking her mother's furs and winter clothes down from the attic and the summer clothes up the awkward ladder, which she couldn't do to her mother's satisfaction, so it was to be left till her father was better. Or taking her to the bank to deposit a check, which couldn't be done through the drive thru, or at the teller's window, but must involve sitting down with a bank manager in his office.

Cancer occupied this bright new senior living house. The disease that her mother and aunt talked about back in the kitchen on Crossbrook Road. So, there were trips up north to the doctors they knew and who believed her fathers recurred throat cancer could be treated, while the doctors down here in this inferior part of the state where the pines and the deer were stunted and people were believed to have a lower IQ, were dismissive and believed, like her, that he was dying. She would drive, too slowly, her mother complained, the two-hour trip back to these sympathetic doctors they loved. The slow driving, she tried to tell her mother was because she had brought bunch of points with her from a speeding ticket on the Massachusetts Pike and couldn't afford any more points. They would eat at a nice restaurant in Morristown and her father would pay, and she would feel like a thirteen-year-old again. Her father was concerned about her having had three jobs in eight years, where he had worked fifty years at the same beloved RCA Victor. She had to keep assuring him and the state unemployment people that she was looking, she was looking. Most days, she ate her dinner with them at home.

Besides these duties, she kept working on six years of sobriety by finding meetings. Her parents' village was westward, nearly into the Pinelands, sandy flatlands of stunted pines and mysterious sugar sand paths winding into their forests. These meetings she knew from former visits. AA meetings, she had found, were like Chinese restaurants, alike all over the country.

One night she drove from her parents' to a meeting the booklet suggested, an evening meeting at a detox out on Beckerville Road. It was still light when she started down the lonely road. The stunted pines reminded her of deformed children, lifting up their twisted limbs in supplication. She passed some farms, nothing that looked like a detox. By the time she reached the end of the road, it was dark, the supplicating pines were silhouetted against a crazily tilted half-moon. Who knew this state had such a road as Beckerville Road?

She found meetings then in Toms River churches' basements, more reassuring, but her heart was still sore from being fired, she had lost her early attachment to these places.

There was also the fact that she left her parents' house feeling like a thirteen-year-old. To struggle against this, she took a coffee commitment at a Three Step Meeting at a rehab near the hospital. When things got stale, she had learned, you took a commitment. This involved taking the big AA urn home with her and bringing it back to set up in the big rehab kitchen. She simply kept it in her car, rolling around in the trunk to remind her she was a drunk. Quickly, the place became a refuge. She went at five pm and bought her dinner there, at cost, from the rehab. Then she sat in the big dining hall with the people in wheelchairs to eat the food she found delicious, feeling grateful that unlike her unfortunate companions, she had a brain that worked and could walk. At seven, she would set up big urn in the empty kitchen and make the coffee. Here, she finally said she was a weak newcomer, grateful she hadn't taken a drink, and people shouted 'keep coming' and hugged her after the meeting.

The other thing she did was join a choir at the Methodist Church just down the street from her room at the painter's house. It wasn't a very good choir and there wasn't the passion for choral music she had in her Congregational Church in Massachusetts in whose basement she had first met with the Early Christians of AA, then gone upstairs to join a dying congregation of the people who preserved the silver service and the China dishes of its early wealth as well as the words and the songs of the liturgy and put flesh on AA's

Higher Power. But this choir, whose music mostly came out of Nashville, would have to do if she was going to save herself.

And, also most of these saving days she came home to the painter's house and heated her coffee, the last light of the stealthy sun, coming through the colored panes of the window laying lemon and cherry lozenges against the creamy wall. The holly tree outside scrabbled at the shingles, and she could hear the jingling of the metal gromets of the sails against the masts of the boats down at the marina. She studied the painting of the dented brass cup hanging from the Peto green door with its letters scratched by someone's penknife. It was fall, so there were few bed and breakfast guests, just two lodgers, herself and an overweight young man who had a large room at the other end of the upstairs. When there were guests, the two of them were invited to eat left over pancakes. She attributed years of these pancakes to the increasing girth of this young man. Once there was a wedding and all the hairdryers blowing cut off the electricity.

Joy she found to be a bubbly woman who loved her visitors, and bringing out the family China to entertain the supporters of the symphony, one of her committees. She grew up here, and married a high school football star, divorced him, remarried, went to Florida and returned. Her wealthy sister, Blossom, came down occasionally and bossed her around, instructing her what to plant in the garden. A silver husky with pale blue eyes lived with them, a dog of great dignity and aplomb. She took him out for walks when she could, causing him to fix his blue eyes on her with adoration and to pin her with his muzzle between her legs whenever she came into the kitchen. Ernie, the ex-husband, was often there in the big

176

kitchen. He lived down at the marina on his sailboat. She was invited to a Super bowl party where Joy and Ernie had a huge drunken fight. It was forgotten the next day and Ernie sat calmly in the kitchen drinking coffee. It seemed these fights caused their divorce, but continued tolerably afterward.

She and Joy seldom talked about the paintings or the painter. Her information about the earlier Petos came from the older people in her choir who remembered Joy's mother, Helen, Peto's only child. Some of their relatives, dead now, had even told them stories of the original Petos. How they were poor, borrowed money sometimes. How children carried the paintings around in a wagon and sold them cheap. She continued her study of the house now that she was welcome downstairs. Over a green door in the studio was one original that hadn't been sold, a basin, a pitcher, and a candlestick. Next to it on a shelf were the actual objects. There was also a chunk of plaster with part of a bookshelf painted on it. This was taken out of a mural upstairs in the room next to hers. Why were these pieces being sawn out of the walls and being sold? The insurance is so high, Joy told her. It's all up to Blossom.

To answer her questions, Joy loaned her the book by Wilmerding about her grandfather and she took it up to her room to read in the big bed at night. The streetlight coming through the red and yellow panes laid lozenges on the counterpane. The masts tinkled down at the marina. The great oak outside her window creaked, its branches tickling the cedar shingles. From this book, she learned finally of the early hopes of the couple who came from Philadelphia, purchased this farmland and built the house, designed by Peto himself. Here they doted on their only child, Helen, shared the townspeople's hopes for this Methodist community whose camp meetings, where the painter who was also a musician played the cornet, drew famous preachers and orators.

He was a good family man and allowed three maiden aunts to live with them at times. Townspeople came to chat with him and watch him paint. He gave lessons to aspiring artists, He built a swing for the child that hung from the rafters of the studio, and a playhouse in the yard. They kept a large garden and some hens. But money was short, winters were long. One demented aunt that lived upstairs and banged on the floor with her cane while he painted. Then came the pain of his Bright's disease that explained the chamber pot attached to the bottom of the Chippendale chair.

And, after his death, there was the widow living on, with the paintings stacked, unwanted in the studio, taking boarders, very occasionally selling a painting to a neighbor, These occasional sales and gifts must have explained the great posthumous injustice this house suffered, far beyond any injustice that had happened to her. That sting was beginning to lessen.

From this book, she learned there was an art critic, named Frankenstein, who was studying Peto's friend and fellow student at the Art Academy in Philadelphia, William Harnett, another still life painter, who had achieved some fame. Why some of his paintings were so different from the polish, the elegant employment of tromp l'oeil of most of them? Harnett was a bit more skillful at this tricky technique than Peto, and his subjects perhaps more appealing to the public. Also, Peto, toward the end of his life, had loosened up his vision and his piles of books were almost studies in abstraction. "Go to Island Heights," Frankenstein was told by an associate.

And so, it was that the critic inquired, as she had, at the local soda fountain, knocked on the Peto green door, as she had, and was welcomed into studio of John Frederick Peto by the mother of Joy. As soon as he saw the battered basins and the stringless violins in the studio, he knew what had happened. The New York gallery owner who had forged the signatures had never been punished.

She found a job. She moved out, but stayed near, in an apartment house that was built right over the strip of fill that had permitted the former island to join the mainland of Toms River. The water of course reasserted itself during floods and the building was sinking so she later had to move out.

A handyman came to repair the painter's house. Not the kind of radical repair it needed. There wasn't money for that. While he was down in the basement, shoring it up, he opened trunks, read old papers, became as intrigued as she, showed her letters he found. "Trunkfuls of stuff," he told her. Joy was fond of him, gave him pancakes, and so he became as attached to the house as she.

There was one last trip up north to the doctor who put seeds of radium around the throat tumor and predicted a cure. A brief time of celebration, she couldn't believe in, and shortly after this the pain took over. It was a tooth, her father said and went to the dentist, who could do nothing. Then the cancer broke through an oozed out of his neck. The odor was terrible. All this her mother reported to the hopeful doctors up north. Yes, finally, they said it. That is cancer, not a tooth. She learned that its turns spiral into ever new depths of horror. Horror turns to numbness.

Hospice was called in so they had some help. A nurse came with a big bottle of morphine. Her father became angry and blamed the local doctors; he wouldn't talk to the hospice social workers. She blamed the Morristown doctors. They gave him false hope rather than preparing him. Most of all, she couldn't help thinking he couldn't let go because he couldn't leave the care of this wife in the hands of this daughter who went about her duties like the sullen moody adolescent he remembered.

Who will store the furs properly now? She thought bitterly, regretted this later when the social worker suggested family therapy, and it was her mother who said, yes, yes! And her father, who exploded in exasperation. She saw suddenly that it was her mother in her fierceness and aggression who wanted a relationship with this daughter so unlike her. And it was her father, whose love of hardware stores she had always shared, whose passivity she had mistaken for love, whose alcoholism and self-absorption resembled her own, who really didn't care.

Her father died shortly after. She was sleeping then in the living room, next to where he slept, while her mother slept the spare room at the far side of the house. The hospice nurse had given them incense to burn to mask the odor. Something woke her and she got up to find her father slumped over the night table. Too late to give comfort, to reconcile, she still regrets this. The nurse came and dumped the bottle of morphine down the drain. This nurse was one of the Early Christians in the basements she had confessed to them, scolded her father for having given up meetings. They both laughed ruefully as the green liquid drained away.

In the days that followed, it became clear that her mother was not a free-standing tower like the famous one at a church in the city where she used to live. She had lost her buttresses.

She had given up driving, was not about to take buses. Didn't know how to use banks, she blamed her father for this. So, it was agreed that she would go to an assisted living place near her brother. The day she drove her to the airport, her mother fretted at how slowly she was driving. Your father never drove so slowly, the ten points for speeding she'd brought with her had yet to be cancelled.

She superstitiously kept up her coffee commitments, the urn rolling around in her trunk, continued to visit Joy, walk Yury. Joy told her the doctors said she had a dangerous erosion in one of her arteries, but she was ignoring it. She didn't even quit smoking. She even made a trip to Spain. Mornings she was chipper as ever, producing her vast breakfasts. But evenings she fought with Ernie.

Then she died, suddenly, during the summer, on a day the painter's house was full of vacationers. They came to the funeral which was held at the Methodist Church and attended by many people. What will become of the house, the neighbors wondered. A realtor was hired by Blossom. The agent's wife was in her choir so she kept her abreast. He would try, he promised, to find a buyer to keep up the house and live in it, but there was the prospect of tearing it all down and selling the lots which was big enough for three properties which could sell for millions of dollars. This thought was devastating to some of them. The little Historic Commission, run by septuagenarians, held little cake sales in the park by the post office, trying to raise money to save it. It was pitiful. There were rich people in Island Heights, but nowhere rich enough. Another great injustice was going to be done to the painter, the painter's house and there was nothing anyone could do about it. All that Pearl, and Helen, and Joy had done to hold on to it was for nothing.

But it was saved. The wealth saved up by the patient poverty of three women, required the vast wealth of billionaires from the ocean front community of Bayhead to be able to preserve it. People came from California. Restoration companies, historians stepped in, and it is a museum now.

She stayed sober, she found a job, and she watched over a period of three years as the major repairs shored up the underpinnings. Metal siding was torn off. Shingles replaced. Experts scraped off layers of paint, that reminded her of the 'dark gravy' that a critic said once reminded him of Thomas Eakins' palette, and found bright orange, tropical turquoise, sky blue, colors the painter had picked out.

And she volunteers now as a receptionist. "I lived here once," she tells visitors.